Beggarman's Cottage

VIVIENNE DOCKERTY

Matador
9 Priory Business Park,
Wistow Road, Kibworth Beauchamp,
Leicestershire. LE8 0RX
Tel: 0116 279 2299
Email: books@troubador.co.uk
Web: www.troubador.co.uk/matador
Twitter: @matadorbooks

ISBN 978 1785890 888

British Library Cataloguing in Publication Data.
A catalogue record for this book is available from the British Library.

Printed and bound in the UK by TJ International, Padstow, Cornwall
Typeset in 11pt Bembo by Troubador Publishing Ltd, Leicester, UK

Matador is an imprint of Troubador Publishing Ltd

I would like to dedicate this book to Judith Ashford and Mary Mackenzie; two lovely sisters and I wish they were mine.

Author's Note

The tumbledown cottage that once stood near the crossroads at the bottom of Mill Hill was like a magnet to me when I was a little girl. Escaping out of the back door of my home on a sunny Saturday morning, my dash for freedom involved running down a track called Limbo Lane at the back of Glenwood Drive, which led past a big dense forest and had a bogeyman waiting to get me behind every tree. The bogeymen never got me, but just in case they were still waiting, I never returned back home that way. Instead I lingered in a hamlet, which I didn't know until I was older was called Irby Heath. The cottage and its grounds became my refuge, where I could eat my crisps and a couple of jam butties, which would keep me going until teatime.

Standing on the boundary of the township of Thurstaston, I had many choices. I could spend my afternoon on Thurstaston Common and take in the beautiful views of the Welsh Hills and the sparkling waters of the River Dee, or walk past the church and manorial hall to the pebbly shore, where lay Sally McCrae's whitewashed cottage in splendid isolation and I could get a drink of pop from the tea shed by the railway station.

My memories of this place inspired me to write my story, *Beggarman's Cottage.* I would like to think that this old tumbledown building, was a haven of peace for anyone seeking sanctuary at a difficult time in their lives.

Chapter One

Alison sat on the stone-flagged floor of the dilapidated cottage, feeling grateful for the pile of old blankets and hessian sacks that someone had left in the corner of the chilly room, even though they reeked of the odour of past occupants. She shivered, though she was warmly dressed in her burgundy winter coat, thick black skirt, black woollen stockings and her black lace-up shoes, which, luckily, she had been wearing before being thrown out of the place she had known as home for the past two years. She wasn't frightened; she had always felt a certain peace here. The old single-storey whitewashed cottage and its grounds had been her playground when she was a child.

It was in the spring of 1967 and the place was called Beggarman's Cottage; a name given to it by the locals who lived in and around the bottom of Mill Hill and were well used to seeing a tramp or a vagrant lingering there. It had previously been a farm worker's cottage, when generations of the Thornton family had tenanted the nearest farm down Arrowe Brook Lane, and was not far from a ruined windmill, which had been knocked down when it was in danger of collapsing in 1898. The acres had once been part of the Arrowe Hall estate when John Ralph Shaw had owned most of the land around, although a lot of it still belonged to the Glegg estate, but by the 1930s, when the years had passed and modern machinery had replaced the need for more than a couple of faithful workers on the mostly arable land, the small derelict cottage had become a shelter for those who had found themselves without a home.

Its sturdy whitewashed walls, the slate roof and four small windows (two at the front and two at the back of the cottage and some without their panes) had endured the elements of time. The moss-covered roof had lost some slates in the winter storms that blew in fiercely from across the Irish Sea and the once sturdy wooden back door that lead to the kitchen, one of three rooms in the cottage's interior, had been kicked in by a frustrated would-be occupant and now hung precariously on one hinge.

It had started raining as Alison had made her way from the housing estate a couple of hours before, where she and her husband, Graham Mason and their ten-month-old son, Connor, lived in a two-bedroom council flat. She had then hurried along the road, past the pub on the corner and, once she had turned into Arrowe Brook Lane, felt thankful that she wasn't far from her destination. With her long brown hair covered with a plastic rain-hood and wearing the pac-a-mac that she always carried in her handbag, she knew she must look a sight, but it was the bruising on her face that she was more conscious of and her need to hide away from prying eyes.

She was missing her little boy already. He would be sitting in his highchair whilst Nana Mason, her mother-in-law, spooned a bit of mash and gravy into his expectant mouth, then followed up with his plastic beaker of Ostermilk. Then his nana would put him to bed in the white railed cot that Alison had managed to buy with a Provident cheque but she wouldn't read him a story, nor even sing to him as Alison did. Then she would close the door on his bedroom if he began to cry, when he suddenly noticed his mummy wasn't there.

Alison got up from the bed of blankets and began to pace the uneven flagged floor, which was covered in a multitude of old dried leaves that had been blown in from the fruit trees in the orchard. Ash within the grate of the wide chimney breast, screwed up paper, bits of glass from the broken window and old cigarette stubs were the detritus of the earlier habitation by human kind. Whilst mouse droppings and spider webs in every corner of the ceiling was evidence that other species were also hoping to make the cottage their home.

She looked at her watch, a little gold one that her parents had given her when she had passed the eleven plus exam and gained entry to West Kirby Grammar School. It was half past six, still light now in the middle of April, although more storm clouds were gathering out at sea. Graham would be home now, as he had been on split shifts that day, working as he did as a bus driver for the Birkenhead Corporation. Her mother-in-law, Nancy, would be telling him that his wife had thrown the towel in and gone back home to those blessed parents of hers.

Though she hadn't, gone back to her parents, that is. Although they lived next door to the tumbledown cottage at a place called Redstone House (a splendid squarely built sandstone two-storey dwelling, with long narrow-leaded windows and a grey slated roof, set in an acre of gardens and woodland) where she would have been much warmer, she had decided to hide herself away for the moment. With the bruising on her face and the depressive state of her mind, it just wouldn't be fair to them, and her father would want to jump in the car and knock her husband into the next century. No, she had made her bed when she married Graham and she must lie in it.

After taking off her rain hood and shaking out her damp hair, she felt in her pocket for the couple of cigarettes she had snatched out of Nancy Mason's packet of Embassy when her back had been turned as she made a cup of tea. Her mother-in-law was always on the cadge when *she'd* run out of money, so this was payback time as far as Alison was concerned. She rummaged through her tatty handbag, which was grubby with age, and found the box of matches she was looking for. Lighting her cigarette, then taking a good long pull on it, she stared out onto the rain-sodden undergrowth in the orchard, not really taking in the charming scene.

Blossom petals, white and pink from the elderly pear, plum and apple trees had created a pretty carpet, and the veggie patch, once a source of food for an earlier occupant, was full of bolted brassicas and fallen fruit from the last season's crop, which had gone rotten and were now all mushy amongst the overgrown weeds.

Graham had promised that he wouldn't raise his hand to her again. Last time he had, she threatened to leave. He had told her that after their little baby was born, he would treat her like a princess, tip up his wage packet unopened, cut down on the booze and visiting the bookies and never shout or be unkind to her again, if she was just willing to give their marriage another go.

He had said that he loved her and he didn't want his wife to have a job. Although her not having a job was the source of all the rows between them, as they were constantly in debt. He was adamant that they were not going to put the baby into a nursery and his mother, Nancy Mason, who they called Nana once Connor was born, would babysit if Alison wanted some time to herself.

And that had been another problem. She hadn't wanted a baby so soon in their two-year-old marriage, hadn't really wanted to wed Graham at all if the truth be told. Any man would have done if he got her away from her dictatorial father, and Nana Mason was a spiteful old bitch, who was always trying to get one over, something that she should have learnt by now.

Take that day for instance. Every Thursday after twelve o'clock, the drivers, clippies and conductors who worked for the bus company would climb up the metal steps to the time office at the depot and a name would be called one by one, records checked, signatures taken and the little brown envelopes handed over to an eager woman or man.

Graham, having worked so many hours that week that she had hardly seen him, was looking forward to a bumper pay packet and had told his mother magnanimously the previous evening, that she could treat herself to an afternoon at bingo on him.

Never mind that he had been served with a notice that if the car payment on the Austin wasn't paid again, the loan company would come and repossess it, or the fact that the Dansette record player and the new carpet that he'd bought on hire purchase wanted paying for as well. Alison was fed up with hiding behind the door on a Friday night when the tally woman came knocking because the pitiful housekeeping that he did give her went mostly on paying the rent.

She paused her tumbling thoughts and threw the finished cigarette stub through the kitchen window, which she had opened to let out the smell of tobacco smoke. She would have to use the toilet, even if it did mean dashing to the outside earth closet in the drizzle and getting soaked, because there was only the rafters left on the outhouse roof. Though she had no option unless she ran along to her parents' home along the lane and she could imagine what would happen if she did so. One look at her face and her dad would be in his lorry, driving down to the flat on the council estate like a man possessed. She would have to wait until the morning, watch him leave for work, then slip in the back way and surprise her mother. It was just a pity that Connor wouldn't be with her, as he loved his granny.

No, Graham had shot his bolt for the last time this morning, Alison mused, as she hovered over the ancient porcelain, which didn't have a toilet seat, and waited for nature to pay its call. Almost at the crack of dawn, Nana Mason had left her three-bedroom council house, a couple of miles away near the Flaybrick cemetery, and had made her way to their flat in an apartment block on the Ford estate. Surprising Alison with the sound of the key in the lock and causing her to tumble out of bed, where she was having a bit of a lie-in whilst her baby slept.

It had been a fraught night with Connor, who was restless because of cutting a couple of teeth; Graham demanding his marital rights even though she was still on her period; and her feeling so depressed because sleep wouldn't come and another day was about to dawn. She knew she would have to repeat the next twenty-four hours the same as always.

Nana Mason had put the kettle on for Connor's bottle, then changed his nappy and fed him whilst Alison had a bath. It was chilly in the flat and she put on her winter skirt and the jumper she had completed knitting a few weeks before, little knowing that she would be glad of its warmth before the day was out.

"To what do I owe the honour?" she had asked her mother-in-law in a sarcastic tone, bringing the kettle back to the boil as she came into the kitchen so that she could make herself a drink. It was her chance to needle the older woman, whom she had never liked, not since the first time she'd met her, although she wouldn't dare to speak like that if Graham had been there. "Your Danny still not got a job and you're on the scrounge again? He's a lazy sod. If I worked for the social I wouldn't give him a farthing."

"As it happens he's got an interview and that's why I got round here early." Nancy Mason's pale face under her brassy peroxide hair looked indignant. "He needs his suit. I thought if I could catch our Graham early enough, I could give him the ticket and then he could call in to Fielden's on his back way home and pick it up for me."

"Well he's not here. He's on a split shift and seeing as it's payday, he'll hang about until the time office opens. Then I suppose he'll treat himself to a nice big fry-up in the canteen."

"I was hoping that he'd get the suit and pay for it, Alison. I don't get me widow's pension until tomorra' and I have to go down to the North End post office to collect it. I haven't even got the bus fare to go into town, unless I can borra' it."

She looked hopefully at her daughter-in-law, her thin, high-cheekboned features arranged into an ingratiating smile.

"Tell you what." Alison had just realised that if she caught up with Graham just as his wages were being handed over, she might get a bigger share of his money from all the overtime. "I'll take the ticket, give it to Graham so he can go to the pawnshop when he's finished work, then I'll do a bit of shopping at the Co-op. That's if you'll look after Connor. Poor love's been teething. I don't mind walking to the depot, it'll do me good."

Freedom for a few hours beckoned and she could always wait around in Birkenhead Park if she was early, as long it didn't start raining rain. It was peaceful in there, with lots of trees and Chinese arches, pretty flowers and bushes in bloom and a nice big lake to sit by.

"Yes, okay. I can take Connor with me to see Pat Benson. She wants me to do some hours in 'er offy shop. Yer know, I think she'll do well havin' that old buildin' next door to the pub turned inta an off-license. Folk don't seem to be drinkin' in the pubs like they used ter."

"Unless their names are Graham and Daniel Mason." Alison couldn't resist saying spitefully, noting the flush under the woman's cheeks as she tried to rein in her temper.

"Well that as may be, took after their father, didn't they? Anyway, shall I mek us a bit of toast? I'll mek it while you get our Connor ready. Put him in that hooded jacket I got him, when I had that win on the bingo. It's chilly outside. Shall I make him a bowl of pobs as well, so I can use what's left of his milk?"

It had been on the chilly side, with the wind whipping in from across the coast at Moreton, when Alison had set off eagerly along the access road from the estate, then turned right past the pub where Graham liked to prop up the bar most nights. She made her way down Vyner Road South, passing the large detached houses in their acre of gardens and the big old manor house, which had been turned into a place for the mentally ill. Although she had heard rumours lately that promiscuous girls were now being sent there.

Promiscuous was the word that her father had called her, when someone told him she was going out with a bus conductor when she was only fifteen. A man of twenty-one who shouldn't have taken advantage of an under-age girl, but her father had soon nipped that relationship in the bud by threatening to give the man a thick ear and report him to the authorities. Alison didn't think that the horrid word 'promiscuous' applied to her. It was love from another human being that she was looking for, even if it had entailed having her virginity taken from her at an early age.

Father always seemed to have had his spies out, just like he had when she found him sitting in his car outside Nana Mason's house in the north end of Birkenhead, a year or so later. How had he known that she was seeing flirtatious Graham Mason, who was tall, dark and handsome, but with not a lot of intelligence between his ears; a bus driver this time, not a conductor – a rise in the status of her boyfriend. She had told no one that she was courting Graham. Not even her younger sister, Linda, who would have thought she was insane to go out with the likes of a bus driver, when she had been given a grammar school education and could have married a man with career prospects instead.

Meandering aimlessly, she checked her watch and saw that she was way too early to meet Graham at the Laird Street depot, so she walked past the Carnarvon Castle, another pub that Graham liked to frequent, looked in the windows of a couple of Claughton shops, then entered the triumphal arch of Birkenhead Park. The park was opened in April 1847; the entrance had been designed by Joseph Paxton, and was full of little hills, wooden bridges and pergolas, rockeries and lakes.

At quarter past twelve, Alison had stood at the bottom of the steel steps waiting for Graham to join her. He hadn't been pleased to see her there judging by the scowl on his face, especially when her appearance caused a lot of jeering from his mates, who were milling around, waiting to be called into the time office. Their heckling had made him feel a fool and no one made a fool of Graham Mason.

His wife had spun him some story about his mother needing to get their Danny's suit out of Fielden's pawnbrokers, had even shown him the ticket as evidence, but he knew that what she was really after was the wage that he had earned that week.

He had told her once, stupidly he thought later, in a moment of passion when she was being stingy with his entitlements that in future he would hand his packet over unopened. Well, she was a silly cow if she'd believed him, because that was never going to happen. Every penny he gave her was down to him. It was him who drove the number 69 bus around the Oxton Circle, or travelled up to Heswall on the number 71, until his bum was numb and his eyes glazed over with the boredom and he needed a drink to reward himself.

If it wasn't for the fact that he had to keep their Connor supplied with his jars of baby food, Farley's rusks and tins of Ostermilk, he'd go on the dole like his brother. Daniel knew exactly how to swing the lead. Alison had made something inside him snap when he saw her waiting at the depot and before he knew it, he had belted her one.

She touched her cheek, still sore, remembering how he had handed her a fiver after he had hit her, then told her to piss off back home like a good little wife. Some of his mates had looked at him horrified, but big Jimmy Foley, someone whom you wouldn't want to meet in a dark alley on a Saturday night, had cheered him on. Wives needed a good hiding now and again and she shouldn't have showed Graham up like she had.

It had all been a blur from that time on, as with tears running down her face with the shock of it, her heart beating so madly that she thought it would spring from her chest, she had stumbled along the pavement in the direction of the flat.

Why do I let it happen? she asked herself, as she lit her last cigarette and stood at the cottage door to let the smoke out. *Why do I put up with the way he treats me, when I don't have to?* It wasn't as if she was tied to Graham for the rest of her life, just because they'd had a child together. She could divorce him, take Connor to live with her parents, get a job to support herself, or go to college and get a few O levels. She had looked at that scenario many times before tonight, thinking herself a fool because she had left the grammar school in her fifth year. She knew now she had done it to spite her father, leaving school without a qualification to her name.

She had never even been in love with Graham Mason. He had been on the rebound from a gorgeous bloke called Andy, who lived in the village above Irwin's grocer shop, but had chosen to go away to university instead of courting her.

One day, as she was waiting at the bus stop in readiness to catch a bus that would take her to Heswall where she worked as a clerk in a garage, still licking her wounds from being dumped by Andy, Graham had opened the window of his cab and asked her to go on a date. He said that Elvis was appearing in *Blue Lagoon* at the Rialto, so as Elvis was her favourite singer, she'd accepted.

He'd been so charming to her then, full of compliments for the way she dressed and wore her hair. Proud as punch that he had a grammar school-educated girlfriend, he was always buying her flowers and telling her how much he loved her. He couldn't wait until they were married and wished that she would name the day. It was her chance to escape her dominant father and he would love her forever if she did.

Graham had changed once the wedding ring had been placed upon her finger. He was hopeless in bed, disrespectful of their married state, never took the time to see if she was enjoying their coupling, had dirty habits like wearing his socks and Y-fronts for days on end and not washing his hands after he'd been to the toilet. He was a street-angel and a house-devil and she was sure she could get him for mental cruelty, because he treated her like an idiot most of the time.

So that is what she was going to do, Alison decided, settling herself back onto the blankets, whilst listening to the faint tapping of the branches on the windowpanes. She'd get herself some legal aid, then divorce the bastard and maybe one day she'd find a man who really showed her that he loved her.

As the wind blew around the orchard eerily and she hugged a smelly blanket to her body, she wished that she'd pinched more than a couple of fags from her mother-in-law. Although if she managed to get some sleep now, she wouldn't have the craving.

Chapter Two

It was around six o'clock the next morning when Alison awoke, her body stiff and aching from sleeping on the stone-flagged floor and in a sitting-up position with her back against the wall. The thrushes, who had made their nests in the boughs of the many fruit trees in the orchard, were singing their little hearts out and as Alison struggled to her feet in an effort to get to the toilet, she could hear the revving of her father's lorry above the birds' refrain.

She shivered as she stumbled out into the dawn, the rain had cleared and there was a fresh smell in the air. She looked at her watch as she returned to the cottage, wishing again that she'd pinched more cigarettes from her mother-in-law's packet, as she was desperate for the comfort of smoking one right now.

There was nothing for it but to sneak across to her childhood home, now that she knew her father had set off for his builder's yard. She'd get warm in front of the wood burning fire in the kitchen, then cadge a piece of toast and a cup of tea from her mother. Her mother would be alarmed as soon as she set eyes upon her daughter, because she would never believe that Graham could be handy with his fists and hit her. Then she'd make her way to the Co-op in Irby village and satisfy her craving for a smoke by buying a packet of Embassy Red.

Her tummy began to rumble as she remembered that the last food she had eaten had been when she had got back to the flat that previous afternoon, only to find that Nana Mason hadn't returned with Connor. After examining her cheek in the bathroom mirror, noting that Graham's signet ring had caused a cut where he had smacked her one, she had treated it with Germoline, then made herself a cup of hot and sweetened tea. Munching on a couple of cream crackers and a slice of cheddar cheese, the last of the block before she did her weekend shopping, she had busied herself preparing tea for the three of them. Sausage and mash was just the thing to please her ill-tempered husband and Connor loved little bits of sausage and mashed up potatoes with gravy too. If it wasn't for her baby, she might have left the bastard this time for belting her one. Wives didn't have to put up with this kind of treatment anymore. Though if she did, she knew she could be homeless. Her parents might not want her back again and it had taken her and Graham quite some time to get on the council housing list. They had only managed to get the flat on the Ford estate, because she had got pregnant with Connor.

Their joyless wedding had been in the registry office at Birkenhead, which neither her parents nor her sister had attended. In fact her mother had gone for a ride on her bicycle to the village, whilst Alison was putting on her newly purchased navy blue and white check suit, which had also been suitable to wear for the office where she worked. Then her father, oddly enough, had driven her in silence to Hamilton Square, where he had dropped her off at the government building, begrudgingly.

There she had made her vows to Graham Mason and only his family and a couple of friends came back to their do, which they held in their two-room attic flat in a Victorian semi on Shrewsbury Road. A plate of ham and cheese sandwiches, some crisps, a sponge cake bought from Sayers, and copious amounts of booze bought in by Graham celebrated the wedding of the happy pair.

There had been nothing for it since the promises of love, honour and obedience had been made, but to stick out the marriage until Connor was old enough to stand on his own two feet without his parents. Although she would have to make sure she hid her birth-control pills. Last time Graham had found them in her handbag, he had flushed them down the loo.

That had been her intention, stick it out for her baby's sake, Alison reflected bitterly, until Nana Mason had stepped out of the lift with a fast asleep Connor in the push-chair and put her key in the lock. There'd been no comment from her as she passed by her daughter-in-law to put the kettle on, after taking her grandson into his bedroom and placing the still sleeping youngster into his cot.

It made Alison's blood boil. Not only because the ignorant woman had failed to say hello to her, but it seemed she was prepared to ignore the cut and the bruising on Alison's cheek as well.

"So, have you nothing to say about what your bloody son's done to me this time?" Alison hissed her question, as she didn't want to wake her baby from his afternoon nap.

"Well, yer must have deserved it, yer always rilin' him. What was it this time? Did yer have a go over the tally woman again?" She lit a cigarette from the packet she had put on the kitchen table and blew the smoke rudely in Alison's direction.

"If you mean did I have a go at him over all his damn debts that I have to pay out of the money he gives me, no I didn't. It was because I'd gone to the depot and showed him up in front of his mates. You should have gone. It was you who wanted money to get Daniel's suit out of the pawn shop and he was narked as hell when he saw me waiting. Anyway, where did you get money to buy your fags with? You were complaining you were broke this morning."

"None of yer business where I got the money from." Nancy waved the packet of cigarettes in front of Alison in a jeering manner. "Graham has a short temper like his dad did. I was always gettin' a belt off him, he broke me jaw once."

"So this is what I have to put up with for the rest of my life?" Alison suddenly felt as if all the fight she had inside her evaporated. She stared at the older woman, noting the early wrinkles on her pasty, creviced face; the peroxide hair that needing bleaching at the roots; the yellowed fingers from too many smokes; and the rubbed up, tatty clothing that the fifty-three-year-old woman wore. This would be her in thirty-odd years – that's if she ever made it to her fifties.

"'Fraid so, unless yer make a run for it. I know he's me son and I know you and I have never got on well with each other, but I'll tell yer now, nothing's going to change. A kid every couple of years and that's if you don't miscarry like many of mine did. Couldn't keep his bloody 'ands off me… Still mustn't speak ill of the dead. It was that year spent in the prison camp that did it."

"Prison camp…?" Alison felt a little faint as she heard Nana Mason's words. She'd not heard of this before. What kind of a family had she married into?

"Durin' the war it was. He went to Burma and the Japs got 'im and made 'im a prisoner of war. He never liked to talk about it, but gone was the nice bloke that he'd been before the call up."

There was a silence as the two women looked at each other. Alison felt a twinge of compassion for the woman who she felt had always despised her, because she had been brought up in a four-bedroom detached in the countryside and gone to grammar school. Nancy Mason had only known poverty and deprivation in the back streets of Birkenhead and had hardly gone to the local school, so she was virtually illiterate. She stood with her hands on her hips waiting for some reaction from her daughter-in-law.

"I'll get Connor." Alison suddenly made up her mind and spat out her intention. "I'm not going to put up with Graham's tempers and the feckless way he treats me over money and suchlike. I'll go to my parents. They'll look after us until I manage to get a job to support us and a place to live."

She turned on her heel. Now that she had decided that she wasn't going to be a bullied wife, nor put up with Graham's sexual harassment anymore, she would take her baby and get out of there, but she hadn't reckoned on Nana Mason.

"Yer won't be takin' our Connor." There was a hint of menace in her voice as she said it and when Alison looked back, there was determined look in the older woman's eyes. "He's a Mason, not a Sheldon and he's not being brought up by people like your bloody parents. He'll become a snob like you and yer sister. He's stayin' here and I'll look after him when Graham's workin', once yer gone."

"I don't think so." Alison was about to leave the room, when suddenly she was propelled towards the window. Her mother-in-law, having shoved her out of the way, rushed into the hallway, grabbed Alison's coat and handbag which were lying across a chair and thrown the front door open. "Go!" she shouted dramatically, tossing Alison's things out onto the landing. "Get out of our bloody lives and leave us to get on with ours."

Nancy made to take a swipe at Alison who had followed her, her face contorted with rage at the thought that her only grandson might be taken from her, her mind full of all the pent up feelings of jealousy that she'd had since her son had brought the bloody girl home.

"You can't do this, it's my flat as much as Graham's. You can't just throw me out without my baby… I'll get a…" Alison's terrified words tailed off as she was pushed hard across the threshold of the flat and the door slammed in her face. As she raised her fist to beat upon it, Connor began to wail.

The bitch was heartless and she hadn't seen it coming, Alison thought morosely, as she wiped the tears from her face with her coat sleeve, with her arms full of longing to be holding her baby close and croon the songs that she helped him fall to sleep with. Nana Mason was a bully and had obviously been waiting for an opportunity to get one over. And she had, big time and how was she going to get her baby from their clutches now?

"Oh gosh, Alison, you gave me such a fright." Slim and petite Catherine Sheldon, dressed in a pale blue sweater and pleated brown skirt, which she had covered with a frilly blue apron, looked over with concern as her elder daughter came through the back door and into the kitchen, where she'd been stirring a saucepan of porridge on the top of the range. "What are you doing here at this time of the morning and where's little Connor? Oh, Alison love, what's happened to your face?" She pushed the saucepan away from the flame and hurried across the room.

"Did Graham do this?" She placed her hands on her daughter's shoulders, looking with concern at the cut that had begun healing and the darkening bruise on her cheek. "When did this happen and where is little Connor?" She looked worried when she realised that her grandson wasn't there. "You've not left him with his father, have you?"

"It's a long story, Mum." Alison felt her legs giving way and she stumbled to take a seat at the well-scrubbed table where Catherine had placed two table mats. "I had a row with Nancy and she threw me out."

"She threw you out?" Alison's mum looked incredulous. "She can't do that, it's your place. Well, Graham's place as well. And what about Connor, he's your little baby? You can't part a mother and her baby just like that… Did Graham know what was happening?"

"No, he wasn't in. Nancy was looking after Connor while I'd gone to the depot to get some money off Graham. You know, before he spent it all as per usual. He slapped me one for showing him up in front of his mates and then when Nana Mason came back from wherever, we had a row about it and she opened the door and flung me out."

"Wait a minute, Alison." Catherine put her hand up to stop her daughter's rambling flow. "When did this happen? You said you went to the depot to get some money from him… that was yesterday."

"Yes, it was yesterday afternoon when it all kicked off and Nana Mason had a go at me. I was just making tea, we were going to have sausage and mash… By the way Mum, can I have some of that porridge? I'm starving."

"In a minute, love, but I have to make sure there's enough for Linda as well." She took a bowl from the free-standing windowed cupboard that was part of the old-fashioned kitchen. A tiled floor, sandstone walls, narrow-leaded windows and an ancient cooking range that had been fitted with gas was what Catherine had to work with, but she didn't mind. She loved living out in the country and still felt grateful that Geoffrey Sheldon had chosen her to be his wife.

"So if it was yesterday, what, yesterday afternoon? Where have you been since then? Did Gaynor take you in? You know, the girl from the flats whom you've become good friends with lately?"

Alison shook her head after her mother had poured out two bowls of porridge from the saucepan, spooned a little honey upon it and came to join her at the table.

"I didn't want to upset her, she's suffered enough lately. Her Harry knocked one of her teeth out last week and now she thinks she looks ugly and Brandon, that's her son, may have the measles. No, I stayed at the cottage next door."

"You mean Beggarman's Cottage? You mean to say you stayed in that hovel all night on your own, instead of coming here where you could have slept in your old bedroom?" Her mother put her spoon back into the porridge, she was too incredulous to eat.

Alison nodded, whilst spooning her breakfast hungrily into her mouth.

"Well, I couldn't have come here, Mum, just think of the scenario. Dad would have leapt into the lorry as soon as he had seen my face and would probably be in handcuffs at Walton Jail, as we speak."

Her mother must have agreed as she didn't comment, just picked up her spoon again and began to eat her porridge thoughtfully.

"Perhaps it's as well. Your dad won't be any wiser, if you go straight home and apologise."

"For what and to whom am I supposed to be apologising to, Mum?" It was Alison's turn to look incredulously at her mother, whose face had suddenly taken on a stern look.

"To your mother-in-law of course. You must have said

something to offend her and Graham must have been cross over something you did."

"Mum. All I did was go down to the depot to get some money off him because it's payday. He was angry because he thought I'd gone to make a show of him and as my reward he gave me a slap in front of his mates. It was bravado from his point of view, keeping the little woman in her place like he always tries to do, and Nana Mason has had it in for me ever since I met her – you know that! She thinks we're snobs, because we live in this place and I had a grammar school education and we've not been brought up in poverty. Not having to live on fresh air, like she's had to do."

"As I told you last time you came home, Alison, you made your vows to Graham on your wedding day and you must abide by them. You had enough warnings from us over his suitability, but you wouldn't listen. You have a baby now who needs you, so you'd better be getting back."

She took the empty bowls into the scullery and Alison could hear the sound of running water as her mother began to rinse them. She also heard her sister, Linda, getting out of bed in the room above.

"I'm not going back, Mum," she called. "I'd rather die than have to go back to that bastard and his mother again." She buttoned up her coat, picked up her handbag and made for the door before her mother had chance to reply to her. There was no way she was going back to Graham Mason and she'd find some other place to sleep if she had to.

A watery sun had appeared when Alison, dodging puddles, walked slowly along Mill Hill Road to the village at Irby. Her body was aching all over, probably from lying on the cottage floor all night. She had hoped that her mother would have been more sympathetic when she saw the state she was in. Well, at least offer the use of the bath, so that she could have a good soak that morning, before being ordered back to Graham to live in fear of him. Because that would be how she would feel, if she went back with her tail between her legs. He would see her return as a weakness and then where the hell would she be?

She wondered, as she past her aunt and uncle's house, the couple having moved into the newly built three-bedroom semi with their only daughter a few months before, whether they would be willing to give her shelter for a few nights. She saw that the curtains were closed upstairs and remembered that her mother's brother was a night-shift worker. But there was always Aunty Brenda who might be willing to help her. She lived in a bungalow near the top of the hill, across from Manor Road.

She reflected on the treatment that she had received when she had walked into the police station at Upton the day before. The bobby on the desk hadn't listened. He'd just shaken his head when she showed him her damaged cheek and told her it was a domestic. She was to get back home and get her husband's dinner on, or she might get another belt that evening.

What was it with men? she thought bitterly, as she made her way slowly along the pavement, occasionally glancing into the well-kept gardens of the older houses that had been there all her life and past the small Evangelist church, where she and her sister had been sent to Sunday school by her mother. Men always seemed to want to dominate. She hadn't met one so far that didn't want to run her life. Her dad was a great example. From the time she could walk he had been on at her. On at all of them: her mother, sister, his workers who jumped to his tune or they'd be given their marching orders, and of course herself.

He was a big man; big in stature, big in business and everyone knew Geoff Sheldon around and about, especially at the Irby Club where he had been a member for years. He was distantly related to the family who had first owned the Sheldon Property Company in Neston and that counted for something in their neck of the woods.

In contrast, her mother, slim, petite and the youngest of three siblings, was of a gentler nature, although could get cross if you pushed her temperate personality too far. Alison's mother was another wife who paid lip service to her dictatorial husband, but as she had once pointed out to Alison, that was what wives were supposed to do. Marriage was forever and the vows that you made on your wedding day were for keeps.

Aunt Brenda's bungalow had the outside shutters on, a sure sign that she and Uncle Mike were visiting their daughter, Ann, who lived with her new husband in the wilds of Scotland. Another night at the cottage beckoned, until Alison decided what to do.

Chapter Three

The ghostly figure of Nora MacDermott, who looked like a fine summer mist to an observer's eye, watched from amongst the trees, as Alison came out of the back door of the cottage and made her way down the side of the building to her parents' home next door. So another human being had taken up residence. It was a girl this time, who seemed to be suffering a great deal of misery. A girl just like she used to be, before her life had been taken away in the matter of a heart beat. This had been her home, still was her home, as her spirit would dwell in the four walls of this cottage for eternity.

It had been in the late summer of 1879 when she and her husband Wally, or Walter MacDermott, the name his father had given to be recorded on his birth certificate, had moved into this farm worker's cottage. It was was next to an old windmill where local tenants ground their corn, and just below the crossroads at the bottom of Mill Hill. It was harvest time in the area and many hands were needed to gather the crops in for the farmer.

Farmer Thornton tenanted the farm along Arrowe Brook Lane and mainly grew oats and wheat on his acres, but had quite a few fields of sheep and cattle, for the supply of meat, milk and cheese to the large population of Liverpool and Birkenhead. He had decided to take advantage of some of the many itinerant Irishmen, who had come over from the Emerald Isle to work for the Wirral Railway Line. Now temporarily redundant whilst 'the powers that be' made up their minds on where the various railway extensions were going to be laid across the peninsula, many stayed on to work and were prepared to live rough in the outbuildings, which belonged to the various farms around.

When it had been mentioned to Farmer Thornton, a compassionate man and God-fearing, that Walter had a pregnant wife, he had allowed them to live in a small tied cottage which had just become vacant, so Walter helped with the harvesting and Nora found it to be a pleasant little place.

The previous occupant, Donald Gough, now deceased, who had worked for the tenants of Arrowe Brooke Farm since the early 1840s, had supplemented his meagre wage with the fruit of his trees in the orchard, his gooseberry bushes and the produce that he grew in his vegetable patch. Nora, born in a crowded cottage on the outskirts of Westport in County Mayo, was delighted to be given the chance to put down some roots herself and start her family.

It was all she had wanted to do since she had been married to Walter. Her own home and a brood of children, just like her mother who had given birth to thirteen. Nora had been the second eldest of an uneducated family who spoke mostly Gaelic, whilst Ellen, her older sister, had taken the vows and gone off to a convent up in Dublin.

It had come as a surprise to Nora, to say the least, when Walter MacDermott, a man eleven years older than Nora, had asked her stone-mason father for permission to marry his daughter in St. Mary's Roman Catholic church nearby. She had thought she'd be helping her mammy forever in the raising of her siblings and become a spinster of the parish helping out with charitable things in her spare time.

She knew she wasn't pretty. Her long hair, which she wore in a bun at the back of her head, was mousy, her nose was rather hooky, her eyes were small and rounded and there was always lots of spots on her chin. She had always been passed over at the socials, when the local boys were strutting around in the hope that they'd find a willing girl who was up for a bit of slap and tickle in one of Westport's alleyways. But it seemed that Walter, a thickset man of medium height with the dark looks of being from Spanish descent, had his eyes firmly in her direction. He was after a wife to accompany him across the water to Liverpool.

It appeared that Walter had been given the job of a ganger – the foreman of a gang of navvies, who were heading across the Irish Sea to help with the laying of the English railway lines. It would be a lonely life; being in charge of a group of workmen, who would only want to drink away their wages in the many pubs and taverns that abounded on the streets of the maritime city, so Walter decided that he would need a wife to do a bit of cooking and take care of his physical needs.

Nora found she had no say in this arrangement, agreed both by her father and the parish priest, who reckoned that it was only right that a good Catholic maid of seventeen should be wed. So she said a dutiful farewell to her family, whom she knew she would probably never see or hear from again, because no one amongst them, including herself, could read or write.

Month after month, she obediently complied with her new husband's wishes, putting up with the poor conditions of a dark, damp room in a dilapidated court of houses in the back streets of Liverpool, where the foul-smelling privy was shared with a dozen other tenants and where their only supply of water was an outside pump. They shared their rented room, which hadn't got a fire to do the cooking, with two of Walter's men and as the gang were paid a daily rate, it was all they could afford.

It didn't help that most of Walter's hard-earned shillings were spent in the ale houses that sat on every corner, so that Nora had to live a hand-to-mouth existence, living off a penny loaf of bread, or the occasional meat pie. Sometimes Walter would think to give her a couple of coins, to buy herself something from a dirty café nearby, but mostly she was forced to compete with all the other poor souls who found themselves destitute in the city. Hanging around the market for the leftover food that the traders wouldn't be able to sell next day, Nora became a waif of a girl, unkempt, with tatty clothing, who dreaded her husband's drunken pawing on their mattress.

Nora had come to hate this life that had been forced upon her and the man who would have treated a dog better, as he was inclined to give her a slap if she displeased him. So it had come as something of a relief for Nora when Walter decided to take his men across the River Mersey to the Wirral, where a railway extension was to be laid between the fishing villages of West Kirby and Hoylake. Not that she knew where these wonderful places he kept talking about would be, but he told her that they would be living by the sea and they'd be given somewhere to live this time and she'd be thankful of it.

All she knew was that she'd be getting out of this terrible city, where foreigners were viewed with suspicion, beggars starved in the streets and children died of maladies caused by hunger. And it hadn't helped, when during that previous winter, that there had been regular falls of heavy snow.

After a long trek, beginning with a ride across the river in a small iron steamboat to a place called New Brighton; a tiring walk along the coastline of the beginning of the estuary; and then spending the night sleeping in the sand hills of Hoylake, they were given a wooden shack of their own. One of several near the cliff face of Caldy, which would be used to house the workmen who were to be employed on the laying of the railway line.

With a lovely view across to the Halkyn Mountains and the islands of Hilbre within her sight, it was here in that peaceful beach-side place that Nora's son, Thomas MacDermott, was conceived; the child who would change everything that mattered in her world.

She had been happy there and time had meant very little to a young Irish girl, who had no perception of it anyway. Each morning when she arose to make Walter's breakfast, she would look across the estuary, scanning the shining waters for the little boats that later made their way back to the nearby fishing village and each evening she would watch the sun go down and watch the little boats sail off again in the gathering dusk.

Her husband, more relaxed now that he was living in surroundings more similar to the town he had left behind in Ireland, didn't spend so much of his hard-earned money in the local inns. Though he still liked a beer and was partial to the brew that was served at the nearby Ring O' Bells ale house, he now gave her a little more money from his pay.

He had looked pleased when she told him that she was expecting his child. He was a man of little words, though quick to anger if she upset him in anyway, and like his fellow countryman, he had a liking for the craic and a taste for a tankard of ale.

One late summer afternoon, when the tide was out and squawking seagulls fought each other for the shellfish and crustaceans that the tide had left behind, Nora saw her husband ambling along the seashore towards their home. She had spent most of the day, sweeping out the sand from the floor of the two-room dwelling with a besom, washing a shirt for Walter and one for another man who lived in the shack next door, then walking along to the quayside where she purchased a fish to cook for tea. She was just about to prepare it for baking over the embers of the fire pit that had been provided outside the dwelling, when Walter arrived, earlier than usual.

She couldn't tell from his suntanned face what kind of mood he was in, because he was neither stern nor smiling and she felt quite surprised to see him at this time, as he usually had a drink at an ale house when he finished work.

He looked relaxed, with his black fustian jacket slung over his shoulder and the neckerchief that he usually wore, untied and in his collarless shirt, black waistcoat, brown corduroy trousers and heavy steel-toe-capped boots, he looked every inch a working man. Flinging his jacket into the shack, he went to sit on a rock nearby.

"We're leavin'," he said, in a flat tone of voice, which gave no clue to whether he was sad or happy about the move.

"Oh." Nora didn't like to ask him why, in case he got annoyed and as she didn't have a great command of the English language, it was always better to keep her thoughts to herself. She was totally dependent upon this man, who had taken her away from all she knew, who treated her as if she was the servant and he was the master. It was just how a marriage in the Catholic Church was supposed to be.

She knew no different. Her mother had given birth to a sister or brother for most years that Nora she could remember and if the dinner wasn't on the table as soon as Nora's father had walked through the door, there was holy hell to pay. Walter wasn't any different, although she had only just fallen for a baby after two years of marriage, but then it hadn't been for lack of trying on his part to get her in the family way. It was his duty he had once told her, when she had confided shyly one time when he was about to straddle her, that she was still seeing her monthly 'visitor' and for one moment of epiphany he was struck with a bout of conscience at his use of her, but he soon got over that.

"Bloody railway bosses," Walter continued, this time morosely, as he had quite liked working in the area, with its pleasant views of Wales in the distance and away from the smog of Liverpool.

"We've been told to shift out of here. They don't know whether they're on their arse or their elbow."

"Oh."

"Is that all yer've got ter say on the subject, woman?" Walter kicked a couple of pebbles against the bottom of the sea wall irritably. "They said we can move on ter Chester, where they're laying a line to somewhere else, but I've told them, yer can't walk far now yer expectin'."

Nora kept her mouth shut. She would probably make him angry if she said that she was happy in the little shack or said 'Oh' in answer to him again.

"I was thinkin', how would yer like to live in a farm worker's cottage instead?"

It sounded to Nora as if he had got down the moon and the stars for her and she noticed he was smiling kindly at her for once. Although, he had used the excuse of her being pregnant to his advantage, as there had been a lot of ill feeling locally against his gang of navvies and he quite fancied a change of occupation and to distance himself from them.

"A farm?" she brightened. A farm. There'd be pigs and chickens and cows that she could have fresh milk from and her baby would grow up healthy.

"The man who told us that the railway's stopped 'cos they've run out of money, said that there's a place a few miles from here that's lookin' fer farm workers. I was brought up on a farm. Well me folks worked the acres until it were turned over to rearing sheep that is. So how about it? It'll mek a change, don't yer think?" Nora nodded eagerly.

It was three miles across hilly countryside and along narrow lanes before they reached their destination early next morning. There was just the four of them this time. Sam Riley and Michael Caffrey quite fancied a change of occupation too; they had both worked on farms before the evictions in Ireland, where greedy landlords had turned their acres over to grazing or cereal crops so that they could make more money selling the carcasses of the animals or the grain abroad, than supporting the 'lazy' indigenous. The other men in Walter's gang had decided to go to Chester.

According to Sam, who had been over to spy out the area as soon as he had heard about it and see if the farmer really did want a hand with harvesting and it wasn't just a rumour, the cottage that Walter would be given for him and his pregnant wife, was near a crossroads, close to a quarry, a windmill and a rather splendid residence called Redstone House. There was also a carroty-haired nursemaid called Sadie living there, who might like a courtship if she wasn't spoken for. She had been very obliging with a nice cup of water, when Sam had knocked on the back door for directions, although he kept that information to himself.

One of the lanes at the crossroads led to a place called Greasby, which was a small village with an old manor house, a cattle market, a school, the Coach and Horses Inn and a couple of general stores. Another lane led to where another old manor house stood and a church called St. John the Divine. Though it wasn't a Roman Catholic church, so none of them could attend a place of worship, but according to Walter, who was a Roman Catholic but not a religious man, the other two men didn't mind.

The lane that passed their dwelling would take them to a place called Irby. It was a village up a hill with another old manor house, a blacksmiths and a pub called The Anchor Inn, where Sam had sampled a couple of tankards of excellent ale. He had said that there seemed to be a lot of gentry around about too, just like them in Ireland who lived in their big houses. These feckers also probably lived off the hog of the land and the sweat off their workers' brow.

However, Farmer Thornton who had his farm on Arrowe Brook Lane, had turned out to be a pleasant chap and was offering a wage of twelve shillings for their labours, although Sam wasn't sure if that was for him alone or for all of them.

And life had been pleasant, thought Nora, as she reflected on that time in the small whitewashed cottage, where a climbing rose clung above the lintel and where a previous superstitious tenant had nailed a lucky horse shoe. The place had been fit for a queen when she had lived there, until that tragic day.

Chapter Four

It was a few weeks before the birth of her baby when Nora met Rosemary. She had risen before the cock crowed to cook Walter his breakfast on the trivet, which was fixed upon the iron bars across the cast iron range. She had fried fritters made from a little flour, some mashed potato, a whisked up egg and leftover ham from the night before, in a flat kind of pan, which had been left to use for cooking.

Walter now provided the food they ate. He had brought a small sack of flour from the mill nearby and was able to purchase cheese, milk and portions of meat and bacon from the farmer's wife, if he wanted to because Mrs. Thornton, a robust woman and mother to three young children, sold to the workers and the local cottage dwellers from the farmhouse door.

He said it was to save Nora from carrying, but the deed was done not out of kindness, more told as a threat of how she would be treated if she ventured forth. Walter was well aware of the suspicion of the Irish that abounded amongst the villagers of Greasby and Irby and the heath dwellers nearby.

He had used the warning of their distrust to his advantage, as in truth he was ashamed of her appearance and he didn't want anyone to see the state that she was in. She wore her shoulder-length hair loose and her bulge though not big, strained the seams of her dirty brown ankle-length skirt, which she wore with a high-necked long sleeve blouse open at the last few buttons and a large piece of brown sacking around her thickening waist.

She had long ago grown out of the pretty muslin dress that she had worn to attend mass at her church in Westport and had also been married in. Her scruffy boots were down at heel and she had no underwear, but he wasn't going to spend his hard-earned money on someone he considered to be his chattel, there to warm his bed and put a bit of food on the table each day. With being foreigners from a distant land and not being confident with the language, he knew she wouldn't be making friends with the locals, who were all part of a tight-knit community, so it didn't matter how she looked.

Indeed a fight had broken out at the Coach and Horses, when fingers had been pointed at Walter and his two mates who were drinking there. People were wary of migrant Irishmen, who it appeared had come to take the jobs of the local farm labourers. They had been called 'bog trotters' and told 'to get back to where yer come from' with ribald comments meant for their discomfort and to make them want to go back home. Walter had been angry, as he had lurched into the cottage after closing time one night and had told her that they would be doing just that, as soon as he heard that the train tracks were going to be laid across his homeland.

After Walter had left that morning, Nora washed her face and hands in the bucket of water that he had brought her in from the well, sluiced his plate, soaked the pan and wiped down the kitchen table with an old cloth she used for cleaning. She looked into the scuttle to make sure that there was enough slack for burning in the cooking range, and checked the wick and filled the lamp with oil. She used the besom she kept in the outhouse to sweep the stone-flagged kitchen floor of the crumbs that Walter had dropped whilst eating, then shook out the dirt from the old rag rug outside the kitchen door. It was then she decided to pluck a few leaves from a cabbage that had re-seeded in the vegetable patch and could be simmered in the old iron saucepan.

Her belly was rumbling as she collected her ragged shawl from across a wooden chair, one of four chairs that a previous tenant had lovingly made and thar matched the carved sideboard that she used for storing her precious plates, cutlery and cups in. She was grateful that Donald Gough, the previous occupant, had collected his bits and pieces lovingly over the years, or they would have been eating food with their fingers and off the dock leaves that grew around the door.

Walter hadn't given her anything from his wages for weeks now and so her own food was rationed, a self-imposed solution to her lack of pennies, as it was her duty to keep Walter fed. She hoped he hadn't noticed that his portions were less than he was used to, as she'd been helping herself to a couple of mouthfuls before she served his meals.

If it hadn't have been for those leaves of a few bolted cabbages, the clumps of potatoes and stumpy carrots that continued their growth each year, the gooseberry and blackberry bushes that had spread throughout the orchard and the trees that were dripping with fruit, she might have starved as she nearly might have done in Liverpool. And with her diet having been so poor in the city, on a couple of occasions recently she'd had to pull out a wobbly tooth.

Her one delight now was the daily quart of milk from the milkchurn, given to her by the kindly farmer as he passed the cottage in his horse and cart. Probably urged on to do so by his wife.

The girl, whom she later knew as Rosemary, had been hiding in the boughs of one of the elderly oaks that grew on land between the cottage and Redstone House. Nora had given her a curious glance before she had bent down to inspect one of the cabbages, thin and going yellow, but edible even so. But as she had tried to straighten up, she had fallen on her knees and had sat for a minute trying to get her breath back before she tried to struggle up.

"Dia dhuit," said a gentle voice at the side of her and as she looked up, she saw to her surprise that it was the girl who had been sitting in the tree and looked to be around ten years old. Nora smiled back ruefully and accepted the hand that was held out in assistance and between them she had managed to stand, though felt a little dizzy. The girl had helped her to a chair in the kitchen, poured her a cup of water from the jug that sat on the table and all the time spoke soothingly to Nora in Gaelic; hearing her language spoken by her rescuer had come as a bit of a shock.

It transpired that young Rosemary, recently arrived from a place near Ballina in County Mayo, was the niece of Hannah Dockerty, who lived at Redstone House next door. Her mother, Maggie, was the owner of Sheldon Properties and came over to the village of Neston each summer to check on the company. Each year Rosemary would spend part of her summer vacation at Aunt Hannah's and play with her cousins, John Cornelius and George.

Rosemary had quite a good command of the Gaelic, gleaned from the children with whom she attended the village school at Ballina, and spoke of the cottage that had once belonged to the Widow Dockerty in the countryside where she lived with her mother and her father Johnny. How she loved that place and enjoyed swimming in the river at a place called the Giant's Tub.

Meeting Rosemary was a blessing for Nora, not a native speaker of English and in truth could understand very little of the language at all. It was good to find a friend, even if Rosemary was a lot younger and liked to skip and jump and play hide and seek in the orchard, but Nora felt much happier than she had ever been before.

One day, on a sunny afternoon after Nora had done her chores and was lying on her palliasse resting, her little friend, who seemed to have unlimited freedom to roam around the countryside, knocked on the cottage door and insisted that they take a short walk along the nearby lane in order to show Nora more of the area in which she now lived.

Hesitant before, as she was always worried that she might not find her way back to the cottage again and Walter would have been very angry, Nora seized her chance to go. Passing the fields and dense thickets that lined their way, the two girls soon found themselves on the road that led to Thurstaston Common and to

Norah's surprise, as Rosemary helped her up the rocky sandstone hill, she had a panoramic view of the wondrous place which surrounded her and could see for miles into the distance.

They sat whilst Nora caught her breath, as she was now only a week or so from giving birth, and watched as Rosemary pointed to the shadowy outline of the hills of Wales across the River Dee and to the vast areas of farmland and dark forests far across the peninsular and over to the Irish Sea. She spoke of her mother, a kindly woman called Maggie, who treated her like a grown-up, not a child as some mothers did and Rosemary's cousins, a little older, who attended the parish school at Dawpool and who liked to go fishing in the nearby ponds.

Thomas McDermott came into the world on a rainy morning without any drama. His mother, well used to being on the scene when her mother had given birth to her siblings, had gone to lay on the flagged floor of the tiny bedroom, where she had created a little nest of hessian sacks. She didn't dare spoil the palliasse that the couple slept on and so waited for nature to take its course. With each wave of pain, she rode along with it, fingering her rosary beads and occasionally crying out to Mary, Mother of Jesus, for forbearance in her suffering. At last the wail of her child as he slipped out upon the ragged sacks beneath her, brought her birthing to an end.

She thanked God for the ease of it and for the first child of the family that she was hoping for. Cutting the umbilical cord with the sharp knife she had brought in with her from the kitchen, Nora held little Thomas to her breast whilst the afterbirth expelled. He suckled well and she was glad that her milk came easily and was grateful that the baby clothes and the rags that could be used for soil cloths, which Rosemary had begged, borrowed or stolen from the inhabitants next door, would fit him well.

She would send him to that local school, or to the little place back home if they returned to Ireland, as Walter now wanted them to. Her son would be bright, would learn to read and write and she'd be very proud of him and as she lay there happily planning his future, she hoped that Walter would like their little son too.

The girl had come back and, from her position outside the open cottage door, Nora could see that she had brought a few supplies with her: a blue sleeping bag had now been placed on the pile of blankets, a white plate and cup and saucer, a brightly decorated oil lamp, a large bottle full of water, a loaf of bread, a packet of biscuits, a wedge of cheese and a small block of butter in greaseproof wrapping, which she laid upon the window sill. The furniture and cooking range that had come with the cottage when Nora had lived there a century before had long been taken or used for firewood and likewise the precious plates and cutlery had gone.

A woman arrived. A woman who Nora recognised because she had lived in the house beyond the oak trees where Rosemary had lived in the warm summer days.

"You can't stay here forever," the woman was saying, her gentle tone difficult for Nora to hear. "If your father finds out, he'll be down to see Graham and who knows what will happen once he gets there. There's little Connor to consider as well – you're his mother and you should be thinking about him too."

"I am thinking of him, Mother." Alison raised her voice and cried out in frustration. "I'm going to get a divorce, show Graham and his bitch of a mother that I won't be treated this way. The courts will give me Connor, because I'm his mother and in a couple of days I'll start looking for a job. I've seen a few in the *Birkenhead News* that could be suitable. Then I can find myself somewhere to rent once I've got money of my own."

"Well, just as long as you know I'm not happy about the situation," Catherine chided, as if she was speaking to an angry child, not a grown-up daughter. "You shouldn't be hiding here in this hovel – will you take a look at the state of the place! You should be facing up to the situation by going back home, even if we did tell you not to marry Graham in the first place. But because you did, you should try to make a go of your marriage for Connor's sake, not go running away like you're saying you will. And who would look after Connor if you started working, that's what I'd like to know? Don't look in my direction, because I've enough to do."

"Mum, I know all that. I know I was foolish not to have listened to you and Dad, but just give me a few days to get myself sorted. I don't mind slumming it here until I've got my act together. I used to love hiding in here when I was a little girl."

"Yes, I know you did and I wasn't very happy with that situation either. I used to worry about that tramp that was always hanging about. I once gave him a good talking to."

"You mean Pete. Yes, I have to admit that he was a bit familiar, but I didn't know that what I was doing then was wrong."

"What!" Catherine shuddered, as all sorts of images began to swim before her in her mind.

"No, Mum," Alison backtracked, when she saw that her mother had gone as white as a sheet after hearing her near confession. "It's nothing for you to worry your head about. Just an old man who needed a bit of comfort, that's all."

She reached into her handbag for her cigarettes and matches, as her mother shot out of the back door in embarrassment. Her mother was such an innocent soul.

Alison was dozing. She had wrapped herself up in the sleeping bag, wearing an old pair of her mother's pyjamas and was feeling quite snug. It had been difficult to sleep, what with her mother's angry words buzzing through her head; the thought of Connor crying for her presence; the cheese and bread of her sandwich sitting in her stomach like a heavy lump and the moonlight streaming through the un-curtained windows, causing eerie shadows all around the place.

She could forgive her mother for going on at her like she had. Naive in many ways of the world, Catherine had never even had a boyfriend until Graham had appeared in her life and her mother would never have dreamt of walking out on her husband as she was planning to do. Alison often wondered why a woman of her mother's generation still lived under the oppression of an arrogant man like her father, who still expected constant respect and obedience from his wife. Hadn't Emily Pankhurst and the suffragettes fought for a bit of independence for women a few decades ago?

Talk about her mother pussyfooting and issuing dire warnings. Her father was not to even know that Alison had visited the family home that morning, nor that she had spent the night in the old cottage, next time she came over to visit them. She was to lie low until the bruise on her cheek healed, because goodness knows what Geoffrey would do if he found out.

She had even been reluctant to find her daughter things to make her stay more comfortable, but an old oil lamp and some plain white crockery which had been left in the garden shed, had been given to her under protest. As was the tatty old sleeping bag which was used for covering up an old table in the garage and a pair of thick pyjamas stored in her mother's suitcase, which were only brought out for wear if the winter was severe.

The food that a stressed out Alison had bought from the newly opened Co-op in the village had been kept to the minimum, as a packet of cigarettes was more important to her whilst she was feeling that way. The bottle and the water donated from the kitchen tap, was all her mother had been prepared to offer, in the hope that her daughter would go back to her husband and keep her marriage vows.

Alison awoke from her doze with a start, then sighed in frustration as she realised it still wasn't morning. The moon, still bright, was hanging in the sky beyond the orchard and glancing at her wristwatch, she could see it was only ten minutes to four. A noise, a sort of snivelling, must have caused her to come to her senses, but it sounded more worrying than the snuffling sound of a pig-snout hedgehog when he was making his nocturnal rounds.

So rising to her feet and with every fibre of her body on primeval alert, she tiptoed quietly to the door. Thoughts of a possible intruder cascaded through her mind, as she gingerly placed a foot onto the undergrowth, where bats swarmed above the fruit trees and moths danced merrily in the moonlight.

It wouldn't be Pete, the old man who used to stay there overnight on his way to Neston, after visiting a couple of his cronies who hung about the market at Birkenhead. Pete, born and bred in a fisherman's cottage on the shores of the River Dee estuary seventy-odd years ago, had preferred an itinerant lifestyle to one of trying to make a living from the vagaries of the sea, until his older brother died and he was left the family boat.

No, it wouldn't be Pete. He hadn't been to the cottage for many a year. Alison's mother had seen him off when she had thought that he might be getting a bit too friendly with her seven year old daughter.

A young boy, around the age of thirteen or fourteen, fair-haired and of stocky build, had propped his bike up against the side of the cottage. Tears coursed down his face with relief when he saw that he had found somewhere to shelter. He looked alarmed when he spotted Alison standing in the doorway with her hands on her hips and turned to grab his bike in readiness to push it quickly back to the lane. She whispered, "No," and shook her head, then beckoned him. Hesitantly he followed, as Alison, with her face full of compassion, appeared to be no threat.

His name was Christopher. "But they call me Chris, that is, my mother calls me Chris, my stepfather calls me 'Boy', though not in my mother's hearing." His words had come out haltingly at first, punctuated with a few sobs as if he was casting his mind back to whatever awful episode, had caused him to run away from his home. Alison listened sympathetically after she had coaxed him to sit beside her on the sleeping bag.

"She never should have married him," Chris said fiercely, his accent quite refined as befitted his Cheshire roots. With his tousled hair standing on end as he ran his fingers through it distractedly, he was dressed in well-pressed denim jeans, black plimsolls and a blue zip-up jacket, shivering occasionally as he told his tale and at times his blue eyes glittering with anger.

"There was nothing wrong with Dad, but she got rid of him. He was nice, took me swimming at West Kirby, played football with me in the garden, then one day he sat me down and told me that he was leaving Mum and going to stay with a pal in London. I asked him why? Dad always spoke to me as if I was a grown-up and he told me that Mum had been playing away and he wasn't going to put up with it any longer. I asked a boy at school what did 'playing away' mean? I thought Mum might have gone back to playing hockey like she had when she went to grammar school, but it seems that she was behaving like a female dog and was doing things with other men. Dad left and I wanted to go with him, but he said that I couldn't. I had to stay with Mum."

"Have a biscuit," Alison said gently, feeling out of her depth and not knowing how to comfort the boy. Connor liked to suck on a digestive biscuit and Alison had bought some from the village shop as a matter of course.

"So why the sudden flight, Christopher?" she asked gently, as he finished eating and it seemed that he was going to confide in her more.

"He took his belt to me and she didn't stop him. In fact she gave me a couple of whacks with it as well."

"God!" Alison looked at him in horror. "What had you done to deserve that? I can't imagine that a mother who loved her son would take a belt to him."

"She said I drove her to it." His eyes filled up with tears and they started to dribble down to his chin. He wiped them away angrily with his sleeve and began his story again.

"She had bought me a leather jacket and I left it behind in a cafe in Heswall, where I was having a milkshake with a pal. He asked me why I wasn't wearing it when I got home from town this afternoon, then started saying that I'd probably sold it and had spent the money in an amusement arcade. He told her that

I'd been cheeky to him, that I'd told him to go to hell and that he wasn't my father. So she decided to punish me, by giving me a lesson that I wouldn't forget."

"A bit over the top I think."

"She said I'd pushed her into it. She said that I've been behaving very badly since Nigel, that's her new husband, moved in. I'd had enough and cycled over this way to stay at my grandparents, but by the time I got to their house they'd gone to bed and I didn't like to waken them. I knew of this place. My Dad used to take me for walks down Limbo Lane and over to Greasby, then we would walk back up Mill Hill."

"Oh, I might know your family, I've lived around here all my life." Alison sounded eager. It could be something to tell her mother. They were not the only family here about, who was suffering a bit of strife.

"No, you wouldn't know them," Chris said, hanging his head so that she wouldn't see his distress. He obviously was still loyal to his mother.

"Well, never mind. It'll all come out in the wash, as my mother used to say. Close your eyes for a little while if you can. It will soon be morning."

The boy had gone and Alison wandered listlessly around the orchard. His visit had got her thinking. What if she were to meet someone who treated her son Connor in the same way? What if a new man in her life brought him untold misery? It could happen. Look how her friend Gaynor was treated by Harry, and Brandon wasn't his. Bad things might happen to little Brandon in the future.

Well, she'd just have to get on with her life as a single parent. She didn't have to have a man – they had only used her for their own ends anyway. Except Andy of course, he had always been kind to her. She wondered how he was liking university.

As soon as she'd had her breakfast at her mother's house, she would make her way to town. She would see if she could make an appointment with the manager of a furniture shop in Grange

Road, as she had seen a vacancy advertised in the *Birkenhead News*.

She glanced at her watch. She hadn't heard her father's lorry starting up that morning, although it was weekend so perhaps he was having a lie-in. Perhaps he had walked down the lane to his quarry to check on something, or was loading a few tools onto the back of his truck.

It was then that Alison heard the shouting. Two men quarrelling and her normally quietly spoken mother with her voice raised. Someone was getting an earful from her father. She felt glad it wasn't her. She walked stealthily along the overgrown pathway at the side of the cottage.

The two men in her life stood in the lane outside Redstone House, squaring up as if they were about to start sparring in a boxing match. Her father was already trying to land a couple of punches and Graham, taller by at least five inches, was standing his ground. Her mother was looking on with her arms folded.

"I didn't come here to have a fight with you, Mr. Sheldon." Graham's raised voice reached Alison, as she ran through the gate. "I just want to take my wife home, she belongs with me. I know she's here, she's nowhere else to run to and Connor's been missing her. He's been crying all night."

And those few words about Connor missing her had been enough for Alison, so she gathered her things from the cottage and went back to live in the high-rise flat.

It was later that day that the man from the house next door appeared with one of his workmen. Nora watched as the old door of the cottage was taken off and a new one, a sturdier looking one that they'd been carrying between them, was put into place. Then the panes of glass in the two back windows were replaced, the door locked securely and Beggarman's Cottage was once more left to itself. The work had all been carried out with a sort of grim silence, except for an occasional order given by the boss.

Nora sighed when she heard his words as he walked back along the pathway. "That'll stop her from getting in again and any other bugger who'll try ter. I've a good mind to put the place up for sale or maybe I'll just have it demolished."

The darkness, that floating darkness that appeared just when Nora least expected it, began to swirl and the voices that she had been hearing from the eons of time began again. She was earthbound. Because of grief and her earthly attachments, she must listen to those distant voices in the spirit world for eternity.

The cottage was Nora's sanctuary as it had been for others over the years. There had been an assortment of wretched people who had been glad of the sturdy walls and its protection against whatever had happened in their lives. Trials and tribulations which needed overcoming and had given them the urge to hide away.

Some stayed until the peace of the place had given them respite from whatever problem troubled them and they had felt strong enough to face whatever difficulties lay ahead. She thought of each and every one as she entered the cottage and stood in front of the newly puttied windowpanes. It was her lookout point, overlooking the greenery of the orchard, where her body had been buried and her spirit must remain.

Chapter Five

Just near the site of where the old windmill had stood until the 1890s was a place called Irby Heath. It was popular with large numbers of campers who came to stay in the warmer weather from the nearest town of Birkenhead or city of Liverpool. There were five stone cottages built in the area of the track called Sandy Lane, which ran through to Irby Mill Hill. There was also a number of wooden chalets standing on the surrounding land, so the place became a magnet for those who came to relax and unwind and the cafe just below the crossroads provided afternoon teas and did a roaring trade at the weekends.

With the shore at Thurstaston a twenty-minute walk away, the common with its wonderful view across to Wales and over to the Irish Sea, the island of Hilbre in the middle of the River Dee and the quaint little villages nearby, it was a magnet for the townies looking for a bit of fresh air to breathe.

Summer became a disruptive time and had the locals fuming. Gone was the peace in isolation that the villagers normally enjoyed. Bottles bought from the Anchor Inn lay broken in the roads and hedgerows, noisy louts caused pandemonium and uproar and Beggarman's Cottage attracted more than its share of vandals at that time. From its windowpanes, wilfully broken by ne'er-do-wells and good-for-nothing people who liked to destroy things for the sake of it, to the doors of the cottage kicked in for them to gain access, where some engaged in activities that brought Nora total shame. Scenes of a sinful nature, drunken men and unmarried women in the act of fornication, became commonplace.

Finding that her tranquil abode was now a place of immorality, noise and disorder, Nora retreated to the orchard, there to dwell in her land of swirling darkness and the sounds of many voices from a distant world. There was a new one now. Rosemary, who had died in childbirth in her early twenties, had passed already and was joining with Nora's parents in calling to her.

One morning, just as summer was beginning to wane and the boughs of the trees were weighted down with rosy apples, two dark-haired young men, one wearing the uniform of a local volunteer artillery unit and the other a striped brown suit and a flat tweed cap, walked down the side of the cottage. The back door, swinging drunkenly on its hinges, after being forced open by a couple of youths earlier that summer, even though the owner of the property had secured both front and back doors with thick wooden laths, was open in welcome and the two men who looked rather serious, Nora thought, made their way in.

They squatted at first, deep in a subdued conversation until one of them moved to sit on the pile of hessian sacks and rags near the window. It seemed that the young man in the uniform was the dominant one. Lighting a cigarette, he began to pace the floor irritably, punctuating his words with stabbing motions with his fingers at the listener.

"Now look here, Jack, what is father going to say when he finds out you're a conchie? Our ancestors have always done their duty when it has been asked of them. Even though Father has never served, he'll still expect you to volunteer like I am. He'll turn you off and even worse, the old bugger might even tell the authorities and you'll be shot at dawn, as they say. Come on man, harden up, you must do your duty for king and country!"

"It's all right for you, Lenny, you've always worn a uniform since you joined the junior brigade." The younger man sounded adamant. "You've always wanted to be a soldier since you could walk. You loved to play with a piece of wood, pretending it was a gun and shooting at people. But you know me, I can't even hold my own in an argument. I'm of the opinion that you should turn the other cheek and walk away from violence. There are other ways of reconciling differences and whenever I'm up against it, I like to sail away in Uncle Howard's boat."

"Well, that is as maybe, but you won't get the option to tootle off when you want to if there's a war on. Those Austro-Hungarians are looking for a fight. Asquith will want every fit and able man to join up and give them a good seeing to. Indeed, I hear Lord Derby's talking about recruiting men to join his Liverpool Pal's regiment already, although I'm thinking of joining the 22nd Cheshire regiment myself."

"Well you do that, Lenny, but as you know I've always had a leaning towards the church. I could become a clergyman and pray for the souls of the British soldiers, then I'd be doing my bit too."

"Father will never wear it, he'll think it's an excuse and what about Joycie? She'll go mad if you don't enlist. All her brothers are thinking of doing so. She'll pack you in and no girl will want to know you and anyway, you only went to church because we've been brought up to do so. You'll have to come up with something better than that."

"Flat feet then or poor eyesight. I'm not going to fight in a war, Lenny, whether Joycie packs me in or not. Just because that Sir Edward Grey chappie says we have to defend Belgium, because we have a treaty with them and the Germans'll traipse through there to get to France, is no reason for us to get involved. Let the politicians do the fighting this time, it's them that's spoiling for a war."

The man in the uniform shrugged, then slapped his brother on his back, suddenly with good humour.

"Never mind, Jack, old chap, we'll join up together and I'll watch your back. See I'm a poet and I didn't know it! Jack... your back? Oh, come on mate, let's go home, it's nearly lunchtime."

It was in the February of 1916, when a man, wearing a black trilby on his dark curly-haired head, who was stockily built and dressed in a grey, three-piece, well-cut suit, and wearing a woolly scarf inside a heavy calf-length winter coat, stood outside the back door of the cottage, looking into the shabby interior with a puzzled expression on his face. He had a familiar face to Nora, who looked at him from where she stood by the chimney breast. Perhaps it was the young man who had come to the cottage with his brother a little while ago.

Thomas MacDermott, Nora's grown son, had travelled across the Irish Sea from Dublin a couple of days before. There was unrest in the southern half of Ireland at that time and there was talk of armed rebellion against the British government, especially as the British were at war with Germany. It seemed a good time for the Irish Republic Brotherhood to pursue the dream of an independent Ireland and they were busily planning the Easter Rising of 1916.

It had been many years before, around the time of Thomas's twenty-first birthday, that his Aunt Bridget had told him the truth of the matter, that she was his aunt, not his mammy. She had reared him as one of her own after his father, Walter MacDermott, had brought him to their house in Westport and dumped him. Thomas had only been a little fellow and there had been no explanation of why he had done this from Walter, other than his wife had died in England because of a difficult birth.

It appeared that they had been living in the countryside, in a place called Greasby, which was over the water from Liverpool. His mammy had been buried in the grounds of the Catholic church, where Thomas had been christened and where they had attended Sunday Mass.

Thomas was now in his thirties, had been raised along with Aunt Bridget's seven children, had done well at the elementary school and had won a scholarship to a Dublin college. He'd had no time for marriage and a family; he had been too busy building his career as an architect and proving to any disbelievers in his field that he was just as good as them. So upon hearing from a cousin who was involved in the I.R.B, the Irish Republic Brotherhood, that there were plans afoot to occupy the General Post Office on O'Connell Street, in an effort to take on the British Army and proclaim independence from England, it seemed a good time to take a little vacation and visit this place of his mammy's demise.

He had taken a chance upon trying to cross the Irish Sea at that time in history, as German U-boats were waiting to attack the unwary merchant ships and in May 1915 the R.M.S. Lusitania had been sunk off the Irish coast, after being fired on by a torpedo.

So it was with a sense of relief when Thomas had found himself unscathed on the upper deck of the passenger boat from Dun Laoghaire and had seen the skyline of Liverpool in the distance. Even more so when the vessel docked and he saw his fellow passengers speeding down the gangplank, glad to be back on land.

He had taken his time to admire the striking design of the Royal Liver building on the waterfront, even though there was a bitter wind and he had been glad of his woolly scarf and heavy winter coat. With its two clock towers and mystical Liver Birds and the Cunard headquarters about to be finished that year, both were architecturally magnificent in his eyes. It was easy to overlook the grimness of the dock lands, the mean streets blighted by industry and the layers of grime from the coal fires which burnt in peoples' homes when you looked at the presence of the Mersey Docks and Harbour Board building and the Anglican Cathedral in the distance.

Though the many troopships in the river caused him a bit of alarm and the sight of the platoons of soldiers being marched along the route to the many vessels that awaited their embarkation, made him glad that he was an Irishman and didn't have to lay his life down for a foreign cause.

He had planned to spend a day or two in the city, looking at the wealth of the great edifices that had been built from commercial achievement when Liverpool was still a premier export port, but when enquiring about accommodation at the bed-and-breakfast establishments along the road from Mann Island, he found because of his Irish accent, he had been turned away. Hadn't he seen the sign in the window that said 'No Blacks, No Irish'? Perhaps he could try the Adelphi Hotel, they were a lot more accommodating towards foreigners there.

He had found a small hotel on the way to St.Georges Hall, a fine-looking building in a neo-classical design, which seemed to cater more for gentlemen, commercial travellers and those involved in business and was more genteel than the many places he had seen. But after one night there, feeling restless and anxious to continue with his mission, he had decided to get on a ferryboat that would take him across the River Mersey to Birkenhead.

His destination, being the village of Greasby, was reached by a combination of a ride on Jack Pye's newly started bus service from Singleton Avenue in an open-sided charabanc and the rest of his trip, once he had disembarked near the entrance to Arrowe Hall with its tall iron gates, by shanks's pony.

There he found to his dismay that there wasn't a Catholic church in Greasby as his Aunt Bridget had told him, but a Protestant one called St. John the Divine and that was in a village called Frankby.

Exhausted and feeling rather resentful that he had made this trip on a fool's errand, chasing a dream that would satisfy his need to prove that he had indeed had a mammy called Nora who was buried in a foreign churchyard, he found himself walking along a country lane. As he reached a crossroads, he found that he had the choice of continuing along to a place called Irby, according to the signpost, or going to catch the chara' back to town.

It was strange how the dilapidated cottage seemed to call to him. There it was, surrounded by overhanging bushes, ancient trees and only just visible as he began to pass it by. It looked forlorn, down at heel, needing to be loved by restoration. His architectural mind, imbued by his fondness of stone inherited from his maternal grandfather, was drawn to its shabby exterior, which was in need of a fresh coat of whitewash and which was covered with an expanse of climbing roses at that time.

His legs, tired with all his walking, suddenly seemed to have a will of their own and he found himself staring into the room that had been used as the kitchen. He wandered in and sat upon the pile of sacks and blankets, where little did he know he had stumbled upon the place where he was born.

She knew him then, he was her baby. The child she had clutched to her breast and sung an Irish lullaby. She sang it now. Tura Lura Lura, Tura Lura Lura… She touched his face and smiled when he seemed to hold that touch in his hand for a moment, then she watched as he dozed, worn out by his search for the mother that he would never be meeting on this earth.

The day of her death, when little Thomas had just had his second summer, had been like any other. She had risen early, made Walter his breakfast, boiled the kettle, and washed and dressed her boy, letting him suckle at her breast, as he still seemed to derive a lot of comfort from it. Whilst she cleaned and tidied the cottage, as she usually did each morning, she had let Thomas play in the orchard where he chased after a couple of butterflies.

It was a warm breezy kind of day as they walked along the sandy lane later, passing the windmill where Thomas liked to make whooshing sounds, as he watched the wooden sails go slowly around and passing the pretty sandstone cottages, where she took time to admire the well-stocked gardens with the clumps of flowers and ornamental bushes that she had no names for. She had learnt to say hello to the old woman, who walked her cow along the track and who always made a fuss of little Thomas, and planned to walk him as far as his little legs would allow him, though she usually ended up carrying him home.

It was good to get away from the torment of being married to Walter McDermott even for a little while, though she was nervous of venturing too far in case she got lost and couldn't ask her way back to the cottage. He hadn't become any kinder to her once she had made him a father and he had caused her sorrow, when first he refused to let her have her "churching", the purification of a woman after giving birth and then refused to have her baby christened, because the nearest Catholic churches were too many miles away. He had told her, that now he had been taken on as a full-time farm worker, he was far too tired on a Sunday to make the long journey to St. Winifrede's at Neston or the other one at Birkenhead and she could get Thomas christened back at Westport, when they went back home.

If they ever did. He was still being stingy with his money, as he was saving for the fare back to Ireland and the more he had to wait for that to happen, the more morose he became. Nora missed her family too and couldn't wait to travel back to see them. They would love her little boy as much as she did.

Walter had taken to chastising Thomas, with a smack or a sharp word if the child had been grizzling, which he was apt to do when his wrathful father was around. It was usually past the child's bedtime by the time Walter appeared in the kitchen, demanding to know where his meal was, if it wasn't on the table when he arrived. On this particular evening he had called at the Anchor Inn for some reason, drowned whatever was troubling him with a few pints of beer and so was a little late than normal, when he lurched his way down Sandy Lane. In his absence, she had taken the opportunity to give Thomas some extra playtime, as he'd had his afternoon nap when they had returned from their walk that day.

"That lad should be asleep on his palliasse," he had shouted angrily at Nora, who was busy rinsing some blackberries, which she had picked from some brambles in the orchard earlier. She had looked up at him dully, preparing to expect a blow when he realised that the last of the bread had been shared by her and little Thomas and therefore there was nothing other than blackberries to eat that day.

Thomas had been sitting on the floor in front of the hearth, tapping happily away on the flags with a piece of wood that Nora had whittled into the shape of something that could have been a dog or a rabbit, until his father had come through the door. He began to cry and in hindsight, she should have read the signs, as Walter's face became puce with anger, as so often happened if he was irritated in any way.

"It comes to something when a man can't get a bit of peace when he gets in from his labours," Walter shouted furiously, bending down to smack the little fellow around the head, much to Nora's alarm and sudden outrage. "It'll be different when we get back to Dublin…"

And Nora never found out what was going to happen when they got back to Dublin, because as she went to shield her child from his father's onslaught, Walter knocked her to the ground and she hit her head on the hearth.

It was late the next morning before anyone noticed that Walter MacDermott and his family were missing. Sam, anxious that the farmer didn't discover that one of his labourers hadn't turned up for work when he returned from Birkenhead market that morning after delivering a couple of pigs that he had killed the day before to one of the stalls, had made the excuse that Walter, having been afflicted with the gripes, had slipped home to use the privy and would be back as soon as he could. The farmer, well used to MacDermott, the Irishman, a surly being whom he kept on for the sake of his poor wife and their little child who he had heard were led a dog's life, had nodded and threatened to dock Walter's pay if he wasn't back by dinner time.

By one o' clock Farmer Thornton was becoming increasingly irritated. He was getting ready to begin the harvesting and short-handed, because Michael Caffrey, the other man who had started work with Walter and Sam, had decided to go back to working on the railway tracks, he didn't need a worker with a gippy tummy, who might be ill for a day or two. There was the tedder and the threshing machines that needed checking over, the implements to sharpen and the pitchforks and rakes brought to hand and whilst he was busy doing all that, he needed someone to be doing the hundred and one other things that wanted attention on the farm each day. So Sam was dispatched to seek the fellow out and bring him back quickly.

Sam, a stranger to the cottage because Walter had never encouraged visitors to his home, walked tentatively along to the back door of the dwelling, listening out for the lilt of Irish voices, or the sound of a baby within. He tried the door, feeling nervous, all the time expecting to be greeted by the roaring voice of his countryman, demanding to know why he wasn't working on the farm and why he was standing there in front of him.

But there was silence as he walked through the unlocked door into the chilly kitchen and a strange and eerie feeling began to clutch at his heart and made his flesh all creepy. A couple of cups, plates and a small amount of cutlery were neatly placed upon the table, along with a piece of wood that looked as if it had been amateurishly carved and a handful of blackberries, though some had fallen on the stone-flagged floor and stained the front of the hearth.

The fire in the cast iron range looked as if it been left to die judging by the ashes, which he saw as he lifted the heavy black kettle and the flat roasting pan that were sitting above the iron bars. And as he wandered into the room where two straw filled palliasses were sitting side by side on the floor and were bare of blankets, it hit him then that Walter MacDermott had done a runner back to Dublin, as he always said he would, when he managed to get a few more shillings from his wages saved.

Anxious now, Sam ran along the lane and back to the farmhouse. He was sure to get it in the neck if the farmer thought that there had been a collusion and Sam had just been marking time for Walter MacDermott to make his getaway. Though it could be a blessing, now that the farm worker's cottage had come free again. He could ask the pretty maid from Redstone House, whom he'd started walking out with, to marry him.

♣

Chapter Six

It was the middle of April 1916 when Jack ran along the lane from Thurstaston Road, intent on reaching the cottage by nightfall. A letter had been pushed through the door of the family home in Lower Heswall and it was signed by the members of a faceless tribunal in Chester, telling him that he must report to Walton Prison in Liverpool, where he was to be incarcerated again.

He'd had enough. This would be the third time since the war began that he would spend a term of imprisonment for being a conscientious objector. He was a pacifist, totally opposed to violence or war and was being condemned by the powers that be and punished for it. Surely the newly formed No-Conscription Fellowship that Jack belonged to should have had some say in the way its members were treated by those in authority. The government of that time had agreed to non-combatants being used in a support role to the military, having added a clause to the Conscription Act, but for some reason Jack had been overlooked.

His heavy black boots made no sound on the thick lush undergrowth that now surrounded Beggarman's Cottage and he was soon pushing his way through the door and into the kitchen. This was to be his place of shelter for the next few days. He noticed at once that there had been a recent occupant, as there were a couple of Players dog ends that had been thrown amongst the detritus in the chimney breast since he had been there before. A deserter perhaps, someone else who had no stomach for a war that was not of his choosing, on the receiving end of public hostility and hatred like he had been treated to.

Jack remembered back to the day when he had told his father that he preferred to study at the theological college in North Wales, rather than joining the army as Lenny, his brother, had done. Jack was a couple of years younger than Lenny. Indeed his brother had been walking out with a local girl and there was talk of a wedding on Lenny's next leave, but in August 1914 when the war against Germany had been declared, there had been no rush for an eighteen-year-old to enlist if he didn't want to. Unless of course you were a patriot and imbued with a need to get over to France and whip the Hun's backside as Lenny was. There had been recruitment drives in every town and city throughout the land, with thousands of exhilarated men parading through their streets.

To say that his father, a privately educated man who had gone into banking, was astonished that a son of his preferred to be a man of the cloth rather than fight for his country like every male ancestor had done, was an understatement. His forebears had fought in the Crimean, the Boer War and in some obscure places in India. It was natural for his sons to want to serve their king and country now there was a war on, even if he was too old to do so himself.

"Your mother would have died of shame had she known her younger son wasn't prepared to fight for his country," he had proclaimed, when Jack had tentatively broached the subject of theological college after supper one evening, forgetting that his deceased wife was the daughter of a rector and she was the one who Jack had got his religious views from. "Look at Lenny. At the first whistle he was knocking on the door of the Cheshires, ready to wear the King's uniform and anxious to serve with the rest of our brave men. What a hero. Whereas you… oh, get out of my sight, before I say something I'll regret later."

Though once he had got over his incredulity of the situation, his father let the matter lie, as he was sure that Jack would soon come to his senses. Meantime he would find him a job in banking, until the government brought in conscription of course. He didn't want a preacher for a son and he was sure that Joycie, Jack's young girlfriend, wouldn't want to be a rector's wife either.

When 20,000 casualties had been recorded in the first two weeks after hostilities commenced, including Lenny who died at the Battle of Mons, which was the first major battle defending Belgium after war had been declared, compulsory call up looked increasingly likely and when Jack refused the call to arms that had appeared in a letter on the doormat in early 1915, he was summoned to appear before a tribunal in Chester.

On that designated morning, Jack caught an early train from Heswall Hills station and presented himself at the town hall, where a room had been put aside for the carrying out of the formalities. He was surprised to see that he was not the only man to be asked to the place that day. There were another eight men waiting in the room, beside him. Most were smoking nervously, some sat on chairs with their heads in their hands and others stood resolute. This was their chance to tell these dictators that war was evil and a man should be allowed the freedom of choice on whether he should kill another member of the human race. Which was exactly what Jack told the panel at his interview.

"Thou shalt not kill," was his answer to the question, put to him by one member of the panel who had been a hero in the Boer war and who asked him why he didn't want to fight for his King and Country? "I don't want to carry a gun, I don't want to be involved in armed combat or fight a war that I don't believe in. Look at my brother, for heaven's sake. He died at the Battle of Mons defending the people of Ardennes, so the war isn't even being fought on British soil. I feel passionate enough to stand my ground and follow the commandment in the Bible, that was handed down to us in tablets of stone."

There had been a sharp intake of breath when the panel, mostly made up of businessmen, a couple of wives who were married to serving officers and a town hall dignitary who was ex-military, heard his words and Jack's fate was sealed. And so whilst Lenny had been sent to the front in an effort to become a conquering hero, his brother was being marched away to serve an undefined term of imprisonment in Walton Jail.

The punishment was designed to break the spirit of the pacifist and for six long months Jack was forced to make fertilizer from the bodies of dead animals. A strategy devised to cause anguish to any sensitive man. There was the silence rule, solitary confinement, which also meant Jack wasn't allowed any visitors and was given a diet of water and bread.

A lot of the inmates who had been jailed because of their principles succumbed. Some were sent straight to the battlefront, when on rueful reflection, they decided to ask for a pardon from their imprisonment and were used as gun fodder in the trenches of foreign fields. Others like Jack were recorded as being mentally affected and needing treatment, according to the authorities and would be dealt with in time. And it was true that Jack's belief in God, his faith that the omnipotent being that he had worshipped since childhood and who had not intervened in Europe's armageddon, was somewhat shaken and he felt traumatized.

Andrew Burton was the psychiatrist who was assigned to Jack, when after his release from confinement Jack was sent to a manor house near Willaston, which had been acquired by the government to be used for the treatment of the mentally ill. Electric-shock treatment and medication was the norm for these inmates and there Jack was to stay, until the powers that be decided what to do with him.

The psychiatrist, a young man, not much older than Jack and recently out of medical school, was of the opinion that his patient was a sensitive soul; not suffering with a mental condition at all, just unable to cope with the stress of warfare and the fact that he was grieving for his brother.

He said so in his notes that were passed along to the authorities, but his assessment didn't help Jack's case for exemption from serving. Opinion was still such that every man should be doing his duty over there in the muddy fields of Flanders, even if he did suffer from a sensitive soul. If this man's brother could die for his king and country, so could he. He was labelled a coward, dragged from the security of the mental home and put behind bars again.

This time he was assigned to stitching mailbags, a painful incursion on his fingernails and was despised and hated by the prison guards, who meted out even harsher punishments than before.

He wasn't going back to prison, Jack thought, beginning to feel rather proud of himself because he had remembered this place of refuge where he could hide himself away. Sitting on the pile of sacks, clad in a warm Arran sweater, a pair of brown corduroy trousers, thick socks and walking boots and his heavy coat to hand to throw across him while he slept, he began to go over his plans.

He would steal a boat. Needs must, even if he did suffer with a conscience for the rest of his life, but he was a good sailor, having been tutored in navigating by his uncle who had a yacht moored at the Sailing Club on Heswall Shore. It was the only way he could think of to get him away from the authorities. He knew that there would be one or two vessels at anchor out in the estuary at Thurstaston, so he would strike out for southern Ireland and find somewhere to conceal himself until the end of this stupid war.

The young man, who now lay sleeping, reminded Nora of Thomas: reminded her of the son who had gone away. Gone away forever and never knowing the love of his long-dead mammy. She caressed the young man's face, where shadows of recently healed wounds from the fists of bullying prison guards showed up starkly, as the moon above the orchard cast light around the room.

It was after dark the next day, when Jack decided to make a run for it. 'His spirit was willing, but his flesh was weak' had been the proverb that kept flashing through the turmoil of his mind, as he contemplated the mission ahead of him and so he spent the day in the peaceful environs of Beggarman's Cottage whilst awaiting the return of his energy in order to carry out his plan.

No one was going to find him there in the isolated cottage, he thought, as he munched on a ham sandwich, one of many that their daily housekeeper had prepared in readiness for lunch, along with a few scones packed into his knapsack, and a bottle of homemade lemonade. The cottage was out of sight from the lane, screened as it was by a line of oak trees and overhanging bushes and there'd been no sound from the garden of Redstone House.

As the sun went down, quite late that evening as dusk came later as the summer approached, he set off to walk to Thurstaston. He was sure that there was no danger to be had on the road that led to the shore because there was only a couple of railway men's cottages near the station and the railway track, and Sally McCrae's Cottage at the bottom of the cliff.

There was a few moments of anxiety, when he heard the thud of soldier's boots marching along the lane from the train station, but sheltering behind the high hedges that screened a farmer's field full of sleepy dairy cows, he managed to slither down the cliff without detection and stand on the pebbly shore.

He thanked the Lord that his childhood passion had been sailing and so he knew how to handle a boat. There were three vessels that were anchored a few yards away from the shore in that isolated part of the estuary and so he chose the one that looked most sturdy with a mast. The tide was running, filling up the channels and soon it was slopping against the large wooden boat, as Jack leapt aboard, after sprinting across the wet ridges of the sand, from his hiding place behind a sand dune, in case he was detected. After he unfurled the sail and waited for the wind to push him in a westerly direction, he set his compass, then sailed across the choppy waters to a place called Bray, on the east coast of Ireland.

Things would have been fine if he had decided to stay put in Bray. Perhaps he could have sold the boat in order to have a little more money in his pocket than he had, or used it to make a living fishing, but intent in reaching Dublin where he could lose himself in a bustling city and maybe one day be able to study at the theological college, he anchored the boat in the harbour and hitched a lift with a drayman, who had been delivering casks of Guinness to the alehouses of the seaside town.

He arrived in the city at the end of April, just as the British Army had brought in a platoon of reinforcements against the rebellious Irish Volunteers. A handful of its members had barricaded themselves inside the General Post Office and were going to be there for at least a week before they surrendered.

Determined to bring Ireland its independence from the British, there was ferocious fighting and many of the leaders were executed later in Kilmainham Jail. And as Jack crossed the O'Connell Bridge and ran along the street, intent in finding shelter from the gunfire, he was fatally shot in the back by a nervous soldier, who was sure he was shooting at a dissident who was running away.

Jack's last thoughts, as he lay dying on that foreign street in Dublin, were that it might have been wiser to have volunteered to fight the Hun and died defending his own country, as his brother Lenny had done.

Chapter Seven

The two young sisters were exhausted as they had walked five miles that day. Running at first, then resting for a few minutes on a grassy verge to get their breath back, all the time looking over their shoulders in case the man from the children's home had come after them. At first they'd crossed the hill at Bidston, staring with round eyes at the observatory that had been built on the crest. The view across the miles of Wirral countryside and over to the Irish Sea, had been astonishing and had helped to take their minds off their plight.

It had been ten-year-old Ingrid, a fair-haired girl who was the spitting image of her father who lived in Sweden, who had first suggested that the pair of them should make a run for it. Older than Olga by three years, she'd had more experience of the treatment meted out over the years by their odious mother, Rita. Rita earned her living on her back in a couple of rented rooms off Conway Street, after falling out with her strict Catholic mother and being shown the door.

No stranger to the Scandinavian seamen who sailed their ships into the Birkenhead Docks, Ingrid, her first born, had been fathered by Jan, who had promised to come back to marry her mother, just as soon as he got his discharge papers in Gothenburg and Olga was the progeny of Olaf, who didn't promise anything, as Olga was the result of a slip up in the prevention of a pregnancy.

After Ingrid's birth in 1923, their mother had decided to provide warmth and a bit of home comfort to more lonely sailors from across the sea and as word got around amongst the homesick crews, she became a port of call for many of them.

The little girls became an unwelcome inconvenience. At first when they were tiny and she could pass them off as her nieces, whom she was looking after whilst her sister was giving birth to another, she had kept them clean and well-fed from the quite lucrative money that she earned from the sailors. But as they grew older and her looks caused her patrons to haggle over the money she was charging, her manner towards her daughters became spiteful and intolerant. She saw them as the cause of all her problems, from the bulges of fat on her once slim body, to the lines that appeared on her face.

She began to lash out at her daughters. At first it was Ingrid who was the receiver of her wrath. Olga was still cute and pretty and didn't have a lot to say for herself, but Ingrid was mouthy and would complain if they were hungry. Usually there was nothing for them to eat until another foreign ship tied up, as Rita spent a lot of her money on gin.

Ingrid spent a lot of time lying on a mattress in the bedroom, banned from going to the elementary school nearby until her bruises had subsided, or keeping out of the way of her mother before she was accused of something else that could bring on another slap. Of course if a man was present, the two girls would be sent to walk around the back streets of the town, until he had done the deed and gone away.

One morning, another day when Ingrid hadn't attended school as her eye had been blackened by a blow from her mother that weekend and with Olga also becoming the recipient of her mother's quick temper too, a man in a smart suit, carrying a briefcase and wearing a bowler hat, with a young woman wearing a heavy winter coat and a blue felt bucket hat, appeared on the doorstep.

A woman, who had recently moved into the rooms below and had been horrified to see a trail of foreign sailors climbing up the staircase, heard the mother's raised voice and the pitiful sobbing of the children, had let these people in and it wasn't long before Ingrid and Olga were shepherded out of the house and taken to a place of safety.

According to Miss Berry, the young woman who they saw a lot of over the next two years, it appeared that their mother wasn't a fit person to have custody of them. Although their mother seemed to have a different view and was a frequent visitor at the Cottage Children's Home called Moorland House, demanding to have her daughters back. Ingrid was at a loss to know why this was so, as their mother had once been allowed to take them home for a weekend visit and within an hour she had smacked Olga for nothing more than trailing behind when they had gone to Grange Road to do a bit of shopping. Rita had obviously felt flush and was going to show the 'posh bitch' at the institution that she wasn't short of a bob or two and had taken them to the children's department at Allison's to kit them out for Sunday worship.

Now that dark-haired Olga, a little on the plump side as she was fond of her food, was out of breath and snivelling that she wanted to go back to Moorland House as she was hungry, Ingrid was at a loss whether to turn back or continue on her quest for freedom. If it wasn't for her dutiful conscience she would have left her sister behind, but the thought of leaving seven-year-old Olga on her own to face whatever punishment the superintendent came up with for absconding, was enough to harden her resolve that they must keep on walking.

She knew it was her own fault that they were lost as she had been following signposts that pointed the way to West Kirby, which she thought was on the way to Caldy where their Grandma lived. But for the past few miles there hadn't been any signposts.

"You have to come with me, Olga," she chided gently. "You agreed this morning that we would try to find out where Grandma Collins lives. We can't stay in Moorland House forever. One day someone will come and take us home with them. Or worse still, someone could come and take *you* away and I'll never see you again."

"Or Mam might come." Olga looked scared, remembering back to the time when her mother hadn't fed them for two days as she had run out of money. She'd only been little then, around four or five years or so, but she still remembered that first whack from her mother because she'd complained she was hungry. At Moorland House their share of food was small, but they were fed three times a day *and* got a piece of bread and butter at supper time. "I like it where we are though, Ingrid. Miss Berry's nice and we'll be missing our dinner. We were having meat pie and tadpole pudding today."

"Grandma Collins will feed us when we get there, I'm sure of it." Ingrid was impatient to be off. Olga had already eaten porridge and scrambled egg that morning, she should still be full, the greedy pig.

It was strange how different they were in appearance, considering they were sisters, she thought, as they set off at a slower pace than before, as the track along a farmer's fallow field that Ingrid had decided to cut through and throw off the scent of anyone following, was boggy. Olga was plump now as she'd been having regular meals at the children's home for the past two years and herself as thin as a rake, or so Miss Berry said. Olga with her dark curly hair, cropped short behind her ears, as the superintendent made sure the children were free of nits in the ten-bedroom dwelling he ran and she, fair-skinned with blonde hair and cut into a short bob, didn't look alike at all.

They both wore brown, long-sleeved dresses and a white pinafore under their heavy brown winter coats, with white knee-length socks and black lace-up shoes. Besides being a place of shelter for unfortunate young children, they were also given an education in another building in Moorland's extensive grounds.

Ingrid reflected on the reason she had decided this morning that they should make a bolt for it. It had been after dinner the day before, when she had seen her mother walking up the driveway with a man on her arm. From her position behind the coat stand in the wood panelled hallway, she had heard her mother make an introduction. It appeared to the listening Ingrid, that a Mr. Atkinson, a thickset man who looked to be a lot older than her mother, had recently married her and that they had come to get her daughters and take them home.

She couldn't hear more, as the door to the superintendent's study had been closed once the pair had accompanied him into it, but she had felt a sense of uneasiness as soon as she had seen them. Something about the couple didn't bode well.

She had lain in her bed in the dormitory later, listening to the quiet breathing of her roommates, as she pondered on the meaning of her mother's arrival that day. This mother who had committed carnal sins with lots of sailors, was cruel and abusive, and had made her illegitimate daughters' lives a misery, was wanting to take them back to her home again. It had come in a flash, that the only person in the world who could make their lives better, was a woman they had met only once, called Grandma Collins.

At the crossroads at the bottom of Mill Hill Road, the dusk began to gather and the girls were glad of their heavy coats because of the chill wind which came across the open fields from Moreton. Olga sat down on a grassy hummock and refused to go on. She didn't remember this 'Grandma Collins' that Ingrid had said they were going to live with and besides, living at the children's home wasn't so bad. You only got shouted at if you didn't behave, or forgot to brush your teeth or wash behind your ears. Olga did all those things without prompting and liked learning how to do a bit of cooking and keep her part of her bedroom clean.

"But it isn't far Olga," Ingrid cried, trying to pull her sister up, but not having the energy. "It's down this hill, I'm sure of it. This is the way we came on the chara', remember?"

Olga shook her head. It had been the year before when Miss Berry had organised a trip to the seaside on a charabanc and she hadn't remembered the journey there at all.

"Are you sure you don't remember Grandma Collins? She came to our house once with our uncle and tried to take us away. She had a big black car and said we could have a ride in it. She said she lived in a big house near the sea."

Olga shook her head and started to weep quietly.

"I know," Ingrid said, pointing to a large house that was just along the road from them. "I'll knock on that door over there and ask which is the road for Caldy? They might even know where our Grandma lives. You stay there and rest and when I find out I'll come and get yer."

Olga nodded, wishing she was lying in her comfortable bed rather than on the grass that might have nettles in it.

"I won't be long and you can see me from where you're sitting."

She walked away, occasionally looking back to check on Olga, until she reached the gate at the front of the property. The house looked empty. Although there were curtains open at the windows, there were no lamps lit against the gathering gloom and no vehicles were parked on the driveway. Ingrid's heart sank; they would have to look for shelter, there was no way they could travel further once it got dark.

It was as she was about to make her back to Olga, that she glimpsed an old cottage a few yards ahead, behind a line of old trees and overhanging bushes. For some reason, some strange eerie feeling, she felt as if she was being drawn towards the place and after walking down the side of the building, because someone had nailed two lengths of wood across the front door to bar access, she found to her surprise that she was in a pretty orchard. Apples hung down from laden boughs and everywhere felt peaceful. Perhaps this cottage would be where they could shelter for the night.

Nora awoke from the darkness, that floating swirling darkness that appeared without warning and voices would call through the eons of time. So here was another wretched soul that needed shelter, someone else who needed time to lick their wounds.

It was a few days later, after Ingrid and Olga had left Beggarman's Cottage and had been reunited with their grandma in Caldy, that a young couple got out of their Rover which they had parked on the driveway of Redstone House, then walked along the lane.

They were smartly dressed, he in a dark striped suit and Homburg hat, the kind of outfit you might wear at a wedding and she in a long blue satin dress with a matching jacket and a little saucer shaped creation on her head. They walked along the side of the cottage and the young woman exclaimed in delight, when she saw the orchard and its many trees and bushes that were bearing fruit.

"Oh, Geoffrey, all this land to go with our beautiful house and look at this dinky little cottage as well. Aren't you lucky that a man you didn't even know, has left you all this in his will?"

The man put his arm around her waist and drew her to him. He kissed her slowly on the lips, then smiled at her tenderly.

"Just the place to bring up our children, Catherine. They'll love it here, with the beautiful garden and the heathland just down the lane. A mile or so to Thurstaston Shore and there's plenty of space for them to run on the common. There's a village up the road where you can do your shopping and we can go for walks as far as Caldy. Or if we want a short walk, we can have a cup of tea and a bun at Bennett's tea shed."

"And how do you feel that you had to change your name to Sheldon, so that you could inherit the land, the quarry and the properties?"

"Not a problem, Catherine, I wasn't keen on being Geoffrey Haines anyway."

Life had been a lonely one for Geoffrey Haines, his given name on the birth certificate. He was a descendent of Seamus Haines, who had crossed the Irish Sea with Maggie and Jack during the potato famine of 1847. Seamus had later worked his way up from cabin boy to head steward on the White Star Shipping Line.

Clarissa, Geoffrey's great-grandmother, whom Seamus had

married late in life, as he preferred to be wedded to his job more than a woman, was to left to her own devices whilst Seamus sailed from Liverpool to New York. Hence, it was a surprise to both of them, when a child was born in 1873. James Clarence Haines, their progeny, became a clerk in the offices of a merchants' warehouse that sold anything and everything from around the world. James married Mary Smith, the daughter of a shopkeeper in Crosby and in 1913 when the war began, the couple moved to the safer environs of the outskirts of Birkenhead with their small son, Geoffrey.

In all those years, it was only the maternal side of the family that Geoffrey had been aware of. His father, James, a strict man who liked to retreat to his study and read his newspaper or one of his many books that he kept on the shelves, didn't have much interest in his only child's upbringing. His mother, a frail lady after giving birth to an only child in her mid-forties and who had to have a char-woman to help clean their three-bedroom semi in Tranmere, sometimes took Geoffrey across the River Mersey on the ferry boat to visit her relatives. This was a huge treat for the lonely boy, as he was able to play with his cousins on the Seaforth sands.

He had felt pleased when one day his father had taken the time to call him into his study, to tell his son about the paternal ancestors, who had come over from Ireland in the 1840s. With a keen interest in genealogy, James had begun to see if he could trace his forebears and as Seamus had died and, him not having been close to his sea-going father, he had decided to see how far back he could go.

It had been a great surprise when one day, having gone to the Town Hall to check the Births, Marriages and Deaths Registers, he found that they were distantly related to a family in Neston, where the head of this dynasty was called Michael Haines.

"See Geoffrey," he had said proudly, showing a certificate to his fourteen-year-old son, who was having to start an apprenticeship with a builder because he hadn't performed very well academically at school. "The head of the Sheldon Property Company for a relation. I looked him up in *Who's Who*."

Then the matter had been forgotten, thought Geoffrey, as he walked around the three rooms of the dilapidated old cottage, promising himself that one day he would either demolish it or make it habitable as a country retreat, until that fateful day when he saw an advertisement published in the *Birkenhead News*.

It had been from a firm of solicitors in Chester, who were looking for any relative or kin of the late Michael Haines of Neston and upon investigation it appeared that amongst the many claimants who applied to the deceased's estate, Geoffrey had a very good case.

Not that he had become a wealthy man overnight. There were strings attached and the estate was large and there were impostors who had suddenly decided that they were related, so the firm of solicitors had taken their time investigating them.

It appeared that there had been two branches to this family. Michael Haines had been the legitimate heir to the Sheldon Company and all its land and properties. Hannah, his stepsister and the by-blow of Michael's father, Jack, had been given Redstone House, the cottage and a nearby quarry by Michael's very forgiving mother, Maggie.

When two of Hannah's boys had died in the Great War and then Hannah in previous years, everything had reverted back to the Sheldon Company. So Geoffrey, proving to be the lawful descendent and willing to change his name, as Michael Haines had insisted in his will that any heirs should do, was given a share of the inheritance.

It had come just in time for Geoffrey. It seemed that Germany was warmongering again and perhaps it wouldn't be long before Britain would have to protect its shores. A man with a building business could go a long way towards avoiding conscription, if he was willing to help in the war effort and that was exactly what Geoffrey decided he must do.

♣

Chapter Eight

It was in the spring of 1940 when a swarthy-looking, heavy-jowled man carrying a rucksack, a rolled up tent and a blanket on his back, came walking along by the side of the cottage. It was growing dusk and it appeared that the man had been hurrying, as his breathing was laboured and sweat was running in rivulets down his cheeks. He wore a brown striped shirt with the sleeves rolled up to his elbows and a pair of black pin-striped trousers above his black, highly polished shoes and over his left arm he carried a winter coat.

With his curling, collar-length hair under a trilby hat and wearing a pair of horn-rimmed spectacles, an onlooker could have wondered why such a well-dressed, middle-aged man would come rushing along the lane, then disappear into the grounds of Beggarman's Cottage. Surely he had got his bearings wrong and he should be knocking next door at Redstone House.

The man in fact was called Joseph Inkerman, a German Jew who earned his living as a pawnbroker from a little shop at the bottom of Hinderton Street, in the nearby town of Birkenhead. A resident there for almost six years, he had come across from Berlin to marry a distant cousin, Dorothy, and her father had set them up in the business as a dowry for his daughter's hand.

Dorothy had been born in Birkenhead, the daughter of a German man who was a goldsmith and who had moved with his wife from their homeland at the outbreak of World War 1. However Joseph, after a wave of xenophobia against men of

German, Austrian origin or of Italian extraction who were living in Britain, was considered an enemy alien now that their homelands were at war.

There were around 80,000 of these likely suspects who might help Britain's enemies in the event of an invasion and so they were summoned to a place of judgment by a panel of judiciaries. If it was decided that the suspect was a High Risk Category A, they would be immediately interned and not released until the British had won the hostilities. If their enemy status was a matter of doubt, a Category B grade would be awarded; a position that was supervised, but the person could still be held in a camp near Huyton, if the tribunal saw it as so. Category C was just a recording of the fact the person were from any of these three enemy countries. Though not a threat to anyone, if you had lived in Britain as long as Dorothy's parents had.

Joseph was frightened. Not being an natural English speaker, as Dorothy and he often spoke Yiddish when they were alone, he knew that his German accent and his lack of understanding of the English language if people spoke to him too quickly, was going to be enough reason for him to be interned. They'd muddle him at the tribunal, make him say things that wasn't true – he might get tortured by the military and even shot. That was what they would do to you in Germany if you were a threat to the security of the country, so in Joseph's terrified opinion, the British authorities could do that too.

So the night before he was due to face what he considered was 'his firing squad,' he had written a mournful note to Dorothy whilst she was sleeping, packed a rucksack with a few spare clothes in and his pen knife, took a tent and a blanket from the pawn shop, helped himself to a couple of bagels and half a dozen gelfilte fish balls from the larder and stole away in the early hours.

In the year that followed the outbreak of the Second World War, many foreigners who had settled in Britain, seeing it to be one of the best and safest places to live, had come under scrutiny. The Italians, who were allies of Germany, had their property and businesses attacked by baying mobs, the Austrians and Germans alike found swastikas painted on their doors. Members of the fascist groups sought out the 'alien' to give them a good kicking and many people were fearful of their lives. Up to now, the Inkerman's had been free of the ignominy and humiliation of being branded a spy or a traitor, as they were needed by the poor to stump up a bit of cash between payday, but it was only a matter of time.

Joseph, mindful of his German identity and fearful of the fact that the panel may choose to have him put away in case he was proven to be an enemy or even worse a possible spy, decided to leave dear Dorothy, a capable lady, to run their business and lie low.

It had been a couple of years before, when Joseph and Dorothy decided to have a well-earned break in the countryside and had hired one of the wooden shacks on Irby heathland. To be free from the smoke and smog which hung over the small row of terrace shops on Borough Road in Birkenhead for a week or so, would be a source of great delight for the pair of them. Dorothy's parents were still fit and active and had a little jewellers shop themselves nearby, so they were happy to keep an eye on the couple's premises whilst they were away.

Joseph sat on the pile of blankets and sacks, after he had chewed on the last of his bagel, ate a fish ball and thought back to that idyllic time on holiday. He had known of this cottage, having passed it by on many an occasion when he and dear Dorothy had taken a walk to Arrowe Park, which had been another place that had given them happiness. With its old stately hall built of gold-coloured stone in 1835, its beautiful parkland, its ornamental lake and a pretty gamekeeper's ivy-covered cottage, the estate had been given by Lord Leverhulme to the Birkenhead Corporation for the benefit of all, the couple had spent a lot of time walking through the grounds. Their favourite place, when they could pretend that they were the only two people left in the world, was down by a fast running brook, where carpets of bluebells lay in the cool of the dark woods and they could listen to the sounds of rooks cawing.

He had passed the entrance to the park earlier that morning, intending to seek refuge in the dense woods beyond the park where he could pitch his tent in isolation, but to his sorrow the ornate iron gates had gone. Being probably used, as they say, for the war effort, although their use in the scheme of things was hard for Joseph to imagine as he plodded by. With lorries, piled high with slabs of concrete and workers standing nearby in readiness, it looked as if the park was being prepared for military use.

He remembered, still feeling hungry, that he and his wife had scrumped many apples from this orchard, after they had tentatively sneaked into the cottage and its grounds one day. They had been curious to know more about this abandoned place, situated as it was behind a line of oak trees and dense bushes and had laughingly agreed that if they ever came into money, they would buy the building, do it up and have it as their countryside retreat.

It was peaceful there; he could rest for a while in the shelter of this sanctuary before making his way to the island of Hilbre, his second choice of refuge, which he had visited with dear Dorothy on their holiday. With its sandstone rocks, the largest of three islands in the middle of the Dee estuary, he could hide amongst the heather, the pink thrift, the yellow birds foot, sea campion and rock sea lavender – all names that Dorothy had identified from her Pocket Book of British Wildflowers, which she had brought along on their holiday for that purpose. He could pitch his tent inside the derelict building on the island and enjoy the sight of the grey Atlantic seals bobbing above the waters and look across to the beautiful hills of Wales.

No one would find him. He could live off fish and the seafood that he would find in the estuary, as surely this war waged by his countrymen couldn't go on for too long. And after his long fearful flight from the authorities, when he hadn't even dared to travel on a Crosville bus in case his presence might be noted, Joseph closed his eyes.

It had been in 1933 when Joseph's parents had received a letter from this distant relative in England enquiring if their sons, Samuel and Joseph had settled down to matrimony. They had heard there was going to be a German Federal Election that year, as President Hindenburg was getting old and with the population suffering unemployment, homelessness and near starvation due to the Great Depression, perhaps one of the sons would like to make their home in England with them.

Many Germans were beginning to fall for the propaganda touted by the Nazi Party and this distant relative, part of the Inkerman family who had fled to England years before because of anti-semitic hate incidents in their homeland, realised that their remaining family in Berlin may well be in peril again. They extended an invitation for one of the sons to marry their daughter, Dorothy.

Samuel, being the elder brother, had settled down with a Jewish girl three months before, but still worked in the family bakery, which had been founded by their parents in Berlin a decade earlier. It had been a profitable business until the Great Depression, but as the years wore on and people began to be affected by unemployment and small businesses were beginning to fail and homelessness was beginning to become a big issue in the German city, it was decided at a family meeting that Joseph should grasp the opportunity of a desirable marriage and go.

Even in the spring of that year, there was cause for a feeling of uneasiness in Germany. There was a restlessness amongst the nation and a feeling of disquiet due to being ruled by the eighty-five-year-old president, who couldn't seem to mend the country's ailments at all. A federal election was to be held that July and a man called Adolf Hitler, a member of the fanatical Nazi Party, seemed to be gathering a lot of support.

If Joseph left Berlin, the family would be sure of refuge in a foreign country, if it ever came that they needed to flee their homeland, as generations of Jewish people had had to do before. Luckily Joseph had found a kindred spirit in Dorothy and although she had never produced a child in the years that they were married, they were happy as they were.

The dream that often haunted him came flooding through his mind as Joseph rested.

His parents, bent and beaten, being driven from their bakery by a mob of starving people and Samuel lying bloodied and broken in the street, shot by a man who wore a Nazi uniform as he dared to defend his family and home. It might have been so, for there had been no communication from his family since Hitler had invaded Czechoslovakia.

When tales of Jews, even though they might not be religious and attend a synagogue, being herded into ghettos and their businesses taken over by local Berliners had come flooding out of Germany, it was a cause of alarm for everyone.

Nora, awoken from her darkness when the man had walked through the cottage door, looked upon his sorrowful face with compassion. He wasn't a stranger, she remembered him from when he and his wife had stood in the cottage, looking around the ramshackle place in wonder. They'd been excited, laughingly planning what they could do should they ever have a lot of money and be able to buy it from the owner. They had kissed a lot and his wife had called him darling and they had made love on the pile of sacks and blankets, although Nora had retreated from the cottage when they began.

Walter had never called her muirin, (darling) she recollected sadly and they had never loved each other joyfully like this couple seemed to do.

As the sun came up next morning, heralding a bright day that brought Joseph a renewal of resolve and purpose, he gathered his things together and went on his way. His intention was to get to the coast as soon as he could, because it might be that the tide was out and he could walk to the island of Hilbre without waiting. He could stay on the island and perhaps in a few days time, if there was no hullaballoo regarding his whereabouts and the tide went out, he could walk across to the Welsh side of the River Dee and hide amongst the forests there.

However, Joseph had reckoned without the presence of the military, or the Home Guard even, whose member was a veteran from World War 1. He was Arthur Morris, a small, thin, bespectacled man, with a face that looked like a weasel; an officious paper shuffler before he retired from a Liverpool based shipping company, he took his duties of guarding the home front from the Jerries very seriously. And when he saw this stranger striding along with some sort of purpose on his mind, Arthur decided to stop him.

Not that Arthur was in uniform. No, he tried to keep his uniform pristine for when he attended the meetings in the community hall. That was when he was not fire-watching, making sure that residents observed the black-out, or keeping an eye out for the return of the Luftwaffes that had bombed Heswall in the previous week. He was wearing a pin-striped suit and a bowler hat and carried a silver-topped walking stick.

The peninsular had seen several sticks of incendiary bombs and landmines being dropped from the sky during the many raids that happened on Merseyside. The prime targets being the docks at Birkenhead and Liverpool and the industrial sites in Bromborough and Ellesmere Port too, but on Mill Hill Road, a landmine had fallen on a field at the rear of a small cottage, blowing out the windows and doors, when a German pilot had jettisoned his load before making his getaway over the sea.

Arthur was always on the lookout for a stranger in case they were a spy, especially as the powers that be were now using the islands in the estuary as decoys. With bricks being hurried over the sands by horse and cart and lots of uniformed personnel milling around, it would have only been a matter of time before Joseph would have been stopped and asked his business anyway.

"I say my man," Arthur challenged when he saw that Joseph, chin all stubbly now and his suit all creased and grubby, was looking in dismay at the rows of barbed wire that had been laid along the fore shore and the tide that was already beginning to creep towards the coastline. "What's your business here? The islands are out of bounds if you were thinking of taking a walk across to them and you'll have to stick to the footpath now because of the barbed wire."

Joseph should have nodded and carried on his way, but he was so overwhelmed to find that his hideaway just across the sands was off limits that he let out a moan of despair.

"Problem lad?" Arthur said it kindly, but had suddenly felt distrustful of this man laden with what appeared to be a tent and rolled up blanket on his back. If he thought he was going to camp out in the sand hills at Hoylake, especially as now there was an Auxiliary Fire Station there and could be an enemy target, he could forget it. There were rolls of barbed wire laid along that part of the coastline as well.

Joseph shook his head feeling helpless. He was aware of the man studying him intently and worried what he should do.

"Hey, you're not one of them conchies, are you? Someone of your age should have been conscripted by now."

"I am not a conchie, Sir..." And in that moment after he had answered, with his confusion causing his heavy German accent to come to the fore, he knew that Arthur Morris would have him locked up somewhere by nightfall and thrown away the key.

On 10th July that year, Joseph was put aboard the H.M.T Dunera, which was anchored at the port of Liverpool. Its destination was Australia, though no one walking up the gangplank was aware of that at the time. Joseph was amongst two and a half thousand detainees, who were people from Austria, Germany and anti-Nazi refugees who had sought sanctuary in England, only to be classified as enemy aliens and were being sent to Sydney. Here they would spend the rest of the war within a prisoner of war internment camp.

Dorothy and her parents had not been told of Joseph's fate.

Indeed no one in his family ever knew what had happened to Joseph Inkerman. He suffered unspeakable treatment from the soldiers aboard the prison ship and those who guarded the inmates below, and never really recovered either physically or emotionally from his ordeal.

With tensions between the Jews, the anti-Nazi's and other suspect German people – a toxic mix of prisoners on board the H.M.T Dunera – and the fear that a torpedo may well blow the ship apart, the soldiers were also on high alert in case of a shipboard riot. The prisoners were made to sleep on the floor, share a soap and towel, had no change of clothing and suffered water rationing in that overcrowded hellhole.

At the beginning of the voyage, Joseph and a few other aliens, had dared to complain about their treatment and that of their fellow passengers, so he became an easy target for the military men. It was the blow to Joseph's head from the end of a rifle butt, coming after regular beatings to shut him up, that caused a concussion and he was hospitalised for the rest of the voyage.

The place seemed strange to Nora in those years after Joseph had gone. Sometimes an old tramp on his way to somewhere visited the cottage, or a man with a scythe swished through the long, green undergrowth. The sounds of the countryside and the occasional shrieks of laughter from the small children next door could be heard, whilst Nora continued her presence there. She seemed to be hearing more voices in that dusky world she lived in. Along with the imploring appeals that she join them from her parents and her youthful friend, poor Rosemary, there seemed to be a familiar voice, whom she couldn't put a name to.

Sometimes she watched as the seasons changed from the lightness of the skies at an early dawn, to the advancement of the darkness in the winter. Spring brought gales when the wind caught the doors and the windows of the cottage and their hinges rattled and moaned. Summer brought the heat of the sun and the orchard grass went yellow and the leaves on the trees were dry. Apples fell in early autumn, plums were blighted and small, and the pears, which were pitted and pock- marked, were pecked by hungry birds. Snow fell early in the winter, bringing a stillness to the frosty air.

Chapter Nine

It was in 1943 before another soul ventured through the cottage doorway. Two souls and one looked familiar. The girl who stood in the kitchen with a young man dressed in the blue-grey uniform of the R.A.F, was a taller version of Ingrid, the girl who had run away from the children's home with her sister.

Her fair hair had been caught up into a fashionable roll, her face was powdered lightly and she wore a little red lipstick on her smiling mouth. Her outfit, which consisted of a tweed jacket over a cream pin-tucked blouse, a flowery cotton skirt and wedge heeled sandals was modern, though rationing of material, clothing and footwear had caused women to adopt the utility look because of wartime. The man, with his dark hair cut in a short back and sides, was very handsome. His name was Frank and Ingrid had met him at a dance, when she had been introduced to him by one of her friends from college.

It had been ten years since Ingrid and her sister Olga had taken refuge inside the walls of Beggarman's Cottage and during that time their Grandma Collins, who lived in a stone-built villa on the main road from Caldy to West Kirby, had been given custody of the girls. They had been brought up as well-behaved young ladies, attending first the local elementary school and then both gaining admission into West Kirby Grammar School. Of their mother, there had been no sign, although their Uncle Stanley, who lived with them, said he had once seen her working on a stall in Birkenhead Market.

When Ingrid was eighteen years old, she had been sent away to a Ladies College to train as a teacher in Chester and one evening when she had gone to a dance at the Grosvenor Hotel, she had met Frank Clancy, the brother of one of her friends. He was stationed at R.A.F Sealand, a base near Queensferry on the way to Wales and he was training to be a pilot.

Ingrid couldn't believe her luck. To have a boyfriend who was both handsome and from a rich family, who lived in a manor house deep in the Cheshire countryside, was the stuff of most girls dreams, but she was troubled by the thoughts of her own lineage and desperate to keep the truth of it from him.

It was a lovely afternoon in July, when Frank decided he would quite like a walk around the area. Free from training to be a pilot on one of the newly introduced Tiger Moths, he craved a little peace from the exhilaration of his working life and all thoughts of the reasons why he was training. It was time to vanquish the Jerries forever and with ground troops in readiness to invade the occupied countries and plans drawn up for a major assault, leave passes from the base where he was stationed were few and far between.

With Ingrid on his arm, in his eyes a very pretty girl with a Nordic look about her and perhaps a candidate to become the wife of a Clancy in the future, the couple wandered along the narrow lanes. It was as they came to the crossroads, that Ingrid remembered the dilapidated cottage that she and her sister had sheltered in all those years before.

Frank was always on about his glorious ancestors. One had been a Lieutenant General and another a Captain in the Rifle Brigade, and he had often asked Ingrid to tell him about the kind of family she was from. He had met Grandma Collins, who was the widow of a local dignitary, and Uncle Stanley, who had been an entrepreneur before he retired from commerce, but only the made up story, the one that had been circulated once Grandma Collins had been given custody, had been given to Frank about the parents of Ingrid and Olga. Ingrid knew that if she was to be a possible Mrs. Clancy, he would have to know a little more. Here was her chance to tell him more of her history, but without the finer details of course.

Frank was bemused as Ingrid dragged him along the lane, past a rather fine old house, where a young woman was rocking a baby in a perambulator on the driveway, whilst telling him in excited tones of their childhood adventure. Once they were inside the cottage, they fell into each other's arms.

"What a hovel," he said in distaste, looking over Ingrid's shoulders at the rubbish that lay on the kitchen floor, the rat droppings, cat's faeces, rotted leaves and bits of paper. Cobwebs hung in every corner and part of the chimney breast had begun to come away, when someone had used a pen knife to chip away at the stone blocks needlessly and a build-up of soot had fallen into the grate.

"What have you brought me here for, you little minx? Are you trying to have your way with me?" He laughed as he said it, but had begun to try and get his hands inside her blouse.

Ingrid blushed and pulled herself out of his arms angrily. "You know I am not that kind of girl, Frank. I brought you here to show you something."

She had always tried to keep herself pure for the man that she would marry and Frank trying it on like that had annoyed her. She wasn't like her mother, who would have taken her knickers off for any man.

"So you're not teasing me then." Frank looked contrite and kissed her on her warm cheek. "Sorry darling, I misunderstood. What was it you wanted to show me?"

"This cottage. This is where Olga and I sheltered when we ran away from the children's home. I told you that we were put there when we were tiny. You know when our parents passed away?"

Frank nodded. "A beastly business, darling. First your father going down with his ship off the Cayman Islands and then your mother dying of a broken heart when she heard. Poor woman. I wonder if *you* would die of a broken heart if anything happened to me. I mean, there is war on, I could be shot down at any time."

He pulled Ingrid back into his arms and began to kiss her on the mouth deeply.

"Whew!" Ingrid came back up for air and began to shove the hair roll back into place, as the hairpins had begun to loosen.

"Don't talk of being shot down, Frank, it gives me the shudders, but are you saying that perhaps our relationship may become permanent one day?"

Ingrid said it meekly, as she didn't want him to think that she was being pushy.

"Do you know, my darling, I think I am. I mean, you're from a good family. Perhaps your pedigree isn't as good as mine, but I am sure my parents would welcome you as my wife. What say, we announce our engagement as soon as possible? Give our families something to celebrate in this time of hostilities." And now that Frank had proposed to Ingrid, there was nothing more to say.

It was a beautiful day in September 1945, when Ingrid and Frank plighted their troth inside a small Norman church near Malpas. It was a grand wedding, considering the austerity forced upon them by the shortages of war, even though Victory in Europe had been celebrated and Frank had returned home a hero. Somehow all the food necessary to impress the guests of an upper-class family appeared on the tables at the wedding reception, which was held in their manorial home. Ingrid, by now accepted by the Clancy family as a welcome addition to their numbers, being now a fully fledged teacher and a pillar of the community having carried out good works amongst the evacuees who had been sent to the area from Liverpool, was highly delighted. Especially as her in-laws had accepted her tragic beginnings.

She decided on that day at Beggarman's Cottage that she wouldn't tell Frank that she'd had a prostitute for a mother and that she and Olga had different parentage. It might have put him off marrying her and what he didn't know wouldn't harm him. She'd had a bit of a wobble when she had been told that she'd need to produce a birth certificate to the Church of England priest for his records, but with her infinite determination that she was going to marry Frank Clancy whether or not, she claimed that as she had been put into an orphanage from an early age, the certificate had been lost.

Grandma Collins, equally determined that her granddaughter was to make this marriage into the Clancy family to cement her fortunes for generations to come, suggested that Ingrid have the replacement certificate sent to her home in Caldy from Somerset House and they could share what had been registered in private with the priest.

It had been a beautiful day when Ingrid had walked back up the church aisle with her new husband Frank and after the wedding photographs had been taken, they made their way to the manorial hall belonging to the Clancy family for the reception. Life would have continued in perfection for Ingrid, if it hadn't have been for the photograph of the happy couple and all the top-drawer guests that appeared in a local magazine.

A favourite past time of Rita Collins, Ingrid's wayward mother was to read the back issues of the up-market Cheshire publication and on this particular day, a year later, in 1946, when peace had been declared both in Europe and the end of the hostilities with Japan, she was flicking through the society pages whilst waiting for the hairdresser to wash off the black hair dye that covered her grey roots. It came as a shock, to say the least, when the bride, a happy-looking Ingrid and, upon further scrutiny, her sister Olga, attired in a bridesmaid's dress, could be seen along with members of the Clancy family, who were long established members of the well-to-do, standing outside a church.

She had to look twice before she could believe that it was her grown-up daughters in the photograph and her heart began to beat rather quickly when she read that the family lived in the deepest wilds of Cheshire on a large country estate.

Her Ingrid, a mouthy little sod if she remembered rightly, who was always arguing the toss with her, seemed to have done very well for herself. And there was Olga as well, who she recalled was the quiet one of the sisters. A cute little thing, who had looked very much like that Olaf fellow, who she reckoned had been the father, looking very trim.

Her past had been forgotten when Rita settled down to married life with Raymond Atkinson, who had treated her like a princess from the start. She had met him after being fed up with the quality of the blokes she was attracting and to make ends meet, she had got herself a job on a market stall that sold bakery goods and where he delivered the bread and cakes. He owned a baker's shop in Exmouth Street and once married she was kept busy being his unlikely help mate, whilst he made a living making his crusty bread.

After accepting Rita's story in the first flush of love, that the girls had been taken off her because she couldn't afford to keep them after her husband had died, he had suggested one day that they would go to the children's home and get her daughters.

Indeed, on that day when the couple had turned up unannounced and was shown into Miss Berry's study all those years ago, Rita had been annoyed to hear that she couldn't just uproot her daughters and take them to live in the rooms above the bakery, she must visit them and get to know them again, before they could be discharged.

Her maternal feelings not really stretching to include being ordered to visit her daughters on a regular basis at that time, Rita waited a couple of years before going back to Moorland House on Ray's suggestion. To her relief, there had been no pitter-patter of tiny feet for the couple and he quite liked the idea of a pair of grateful stepdaughters, who would be now old enough to serve behind the counter of his busy store, which was now selling grocery products as well.

Unfortunately for them, they were told that in Rita's absence, their grandma, Mrs. Collins, had been given custody of Ingrid and Olga and they were now residing at the family home in Caldy. Rita, knowing that money talks and she would have to go through a court battle with her mother and brother to have her daughter's restored to her, decided not to contest the decision and who would want a couple of moody teenagers in their life anyway. She settled down with Ray to enjoy the fruits of his labours.

Therefore Rita was taken aback when she read that Ingrid Collins of Caldy had been married to Frank Clancy from an upper-class family in Cheshire. In fact she had to ask the salon apprentice to fetch her a glass of water, she felt so dizzy at the news. Her babies, the eldest now a married woman and by the look of the outfits of the guests in the picture, she had been joined in matrimony to a chap from a rather posh family and Olga, just by association, would be moving in the very best of circles in society. The question was, how could she benefit from this esteemed marriage as well?

She dressed her slender body in her best and telling her husband that she was going to meet a friend for lunch and he probably wouldn't see her until the evening, Rita caught the train from Woodside to Chester, then continued her journey by bus. She had been to the hairdresser the previous day especially to have her greying roots dyed black again, but with there still being rationing of everything from butter to lengths of dress material in 1946, she had been obliged to wear her blue pleated, utility, two piece suit. Still, it matched her bucket style hat which she had trimmed with a few felt roses that she had found on her recent trip to the market and with her white pin-tucked blouse and block-heel sandals, she felt she looked the part.

The role she was going to play was that of the thankful mother, who had just found out that the daughters who had been lost to her, were living in the Cheshire countryside and she hadn't known. She would pretend that upon seeing a back issue of the *Cheshire Life* magazine, with the wonderful wedding photographs on show, she had made her way with haste to be reunited, as she couldn't bear to be parted from them anymore. The family that Ingrid had married into would surely be very happy and grateful when they met her.

As the train slowly pulled out of Woodside station and passed the shattered buildings of a town that had been bombed by the Luftwaffe in recent years, Rita's mind was firmly on the benefits of being associated with this obviously rich family. She would be invited to all their celebrations: the weddings, the christenings, the birthday parties. Goodness, she'd have to buy herself lots of different outfits when rationing was over. These silly coupons that she'd been issued with would be a thing of the past.

Maybe, just maybe, she'd be given a little house on the estate and she wouldn't have to live with the old man she was married to. Ray was a great provider, what with a thriving bakery that provided the staples of life for a hungry local population, but compared to the world that she would be living in, he wouldn't be her choice.

A few hours later, having caught a bus in Chester, which meandered through country lanes and villages, Rita alighted near the estate belonging to the Clancy family and by this time wished she had stayed at home. She felt exhausted, her suit was crumpled, the powder that she had liberally plastered onto her high-cheekboned face before leaving, made her look haggard and wrinkled, according to her reflection in the compact that she kept in her handbag. And as she applied another coat of vermilion lipstick on the bus, she felt so thirsty and hungry that she could have eaten a plate of wobbly tripe.

It had better be worth all this trouble she had gone to, she thought to herself irritably, as she trundled up the gravel drive, under trees that were still dripping from the last shower of rain, the thinness of the soles of her open-toed shoes, causing her feet to feel damp. Until she rounded the corner, where she saw a manor house in all its glory with a shiny car parked in front and Rita knew then that she had fallen on her feet at last.

Brook Vale Hall, a splendid dwelling, made from local stone and partially covered in trailing ivy, with eight bedrooms situated across two wings and a turreted porch that lead into the entrance hall through a heavy wooden door, had been built in the previous century by an entrepreneurial member of the Clancy family. He had also made his living as a gentleman farmer on the twenty acres of land. A deep, dark forest behind the large ornamental gardens, made it an ideal place for wildlife, where fish thrived in the brook that gave the house its name and gaming birds flourished, which attracted many poachers.

Ingrid, usually out for lunch at this time of day, with her bevy of girlfriends that she had made since becoming a Clancy, was getting herself ready in her comfortably furnished first-floor bedroom, to go out for afternoon tea. No one else was at home, as the daily woman had finished half an hour before, she had seen their old gardener walking down the driveway on his way home as she glanced through her bedroom window, husband Frank was at the family law business in Chester and her parents-in-law, avid breeders of rare cattle, were away somewhere at an auction.

When the tinkling of the old cattle bell could be heard at the front door, as Ingrid was just finishing applying her makeup, she felt a little cross that there was nobody else there to answer it. The family, she knew, could afford a maidservant to do this duty, but because of the war, there was a dearth of young women willing to live in as a servant anymore. She hurried down the stairs, whilst tying the belt of her pretty knee length floral dress, which she wore with white peep toe shoes.

"Yes?" she asked in her carefully moderated tones, which she had perfected over the years since living with Grandma Collins and attending the local grammar school, then she felt her knees begin to buckle and her breath seemed to come in snatches as she saw who was standing at the door!

Her worst nightmare! The woman whom she had hoped that she would never set eyes on again, was there in front of her with a triumphant smile upon her bony face.

"I've found you at last, my darling," Rita cried, launching herself at Ingrid with her arms wide open and tears of joy running down her cheeks.

"What do you mean, you've found me at last?" Ingrid retorted, recovering quickly, shrinking back from her mother's embrace and the smell of cheap scent and sweat that threatened to envelop her senses. " How did you find me? I thought we'd got rid of you years ago!"

She began to tremble inside, as the emotions that were vying with each other to come to the fore began to flood her. There was hatred and disgust for this immoral woman who had given birth to her and sister Olga and according to Grandma Collins, both with different fathers. She also remembered the times when she'd got in the way of her mother's wrath and been beaten for it and recalled the men who came visiting; some kind who gave her sweeties and others who patted her bottom and made remarks that she didn't like to hear.

Then, uppermost in her mind, came the fear that her wonderful life could collapse like a pack of cards if the Clancy family were to meet the woman who stood before her. She'd be caught out in a lie and she didn't think that her in-laws or even Frank, her husband, would tolerate her deceitfulness. Frank would most certainly divorce her, as he was proud of his heritage and was looking forward to becoming a father one day to enhance the family's lineage.

She would have to go back to Caldy with her tail between her legs and her chums at the tennis club, her friends at the Rotary Club Ladies Circle, the congregation at the local Anglican church where the family had a special pew, would all shun her. Just because Rita Collins had come back into her perfect life.

"I saw your picture in the *Cheshire Life* magazine, my darling." Rita continued ingratiatingly. " I know it was a while ago, but I haven't had the opportunity to call on you, as my husband has a very thriving business and it was necessary that I be there to help him." (She didn't say that she'd had to scrimp and save for the fare, as Ray liked to know where every penny went and she hadn't wanted to tell him what she was up to.) "Does Olga live here too?"

Rita stood at the bottom of the stairs now, having shut the front door behind her and was looking about the oak-wood-floored hall speculatively. The furniture looked worth a bob or two even in that room, with its heavy oak table whereupon an expensive vase full of hot-house flowers stood and would you believe it, there was a black fluted telephone sitting beside it and a large gold-surround mirror hanging on the expensively papered walls. There were also a couple of paintings on display of the Cheshire countryside.

"No, she lives with Grandma Collins," Ingrid replied, as she stood there still in a state of shock, whilst wondering what on earth she was going to do with this unwanted relative. Give the woman a cup of tea and see her on her way? Offer her a bribe so that she wouldn't come back again?

The clothes her mother was wearing and the way her dyed hair was rolled under that ridiculous hat and the made-up face that was showing signs of her earlier life of debauchery, wouldn't go down well with the Clancy family if they were to meet her. And Olga would die of shame, if the appearance of her long-forgotten mother affected her relationship with the son of a local man, who had a large portfolio of properties and whom she was going to marry next year.

"Perhaps you could arrange for Olga and me to meet, Ingrid?" Rita's mouth twisted bitterly, as if she was sensing that this posh-sounding girl wasn't best pleased to have her mother standing before her. "I'm sure the little sweetheart will be just as pleased as you are to see her dear old mother again. Anyroad, aren't you going to show me around this palatial palace that you've found yourself living in? Let's start with the upstairs, shall we, and you can show me where to find the lavatory."

Ingrid nodded dully, her heart still beating painfully, as she considered how long it would be before someone from the family, came back home again. She looked at her watch, a little gold one on a pretty bracelet, which Grandma Collins had given her on her twenty-first birthday. Her grandma would be devastated if her wayward prostitute of a daughter began to wreck their well-ordered lives. "I'll have to telephone one of my friends first. I was meeting a few of them for afternoon tea and so I will let them know that I am going to be late."

She moved towards the telephone and Rita, desperate to urinate, began to ascend the wooden stairs, which were covered in a red and black patterned carpet runner, with brass stair rods to keep it in place. "The lavatory's on the right. It's separate from the bathroom, just along the corridor."

"Righteo! I'll have a bit of a snoop when I've finished. I've never been to anywhere so grand."

I bet you haven't, Ingrid thought spitefully, as she asked the operator to put her through to her friend Daphne's telephone number, then found that she must have left already, judging by the fact that there was no reply to her call. She would probably be on her way to the restaurant, where they had arranged to meet.

She swore angrily, trying to keep her annoyance under wraps, as she didn't want her mother to suspect that she only felt hostility at their reunion. The woman might get difficult, if she thought that her daughter didn't want her in her life.

"You've certainly fallen on your feet, my darling," Rita said sweetly, after Ingrid had shown her around the four bedrooms in that wing of the house, which had been given to the young married couple to start their married lives in and noted that every room was resplendent with expensive furnishings. The master bedroom had a walk-in wardrobe, which was full of Ingrid's many clothes. "It's all very different from the hovel that I was forced to live in, when your grandma threw me out. It was a terrible place to have to bring up you and Olga, but we managed somehow, didn't we? If it hadn't have been for that nosy cow downstairs telling the authorities that I entertained men for a living, we would never have been parted, Ingrid. Instead you had to be brought up in a children's home without me, because of her. I'm sorry darling, I did try to provide you with a home when I married Raymond, but my mother had got to you already. What must you think of me?"

She could tell from Ingrid's face that her re-appearance in her daughter's life had not been greeted in the manner that she had expected, but the girl would have to get used to it. There was no way that Rita was going to miss out on a chance of rubbing shoulders with members of high society, even if she had to resort to blackmail. She was sure that the Clancy family wouldn't be happy with the truth of their daughter-in-law's beginnings and she could use that to her advantage, if Ingrid was considering other ideas.

"Now why don't you show me around the rooms downstairs," Rita said briskly, moving to stand at the top of the stairs whilst she was speaking. "And then you can get someone to make me a pot of tea and perhaps a slice of cake and we can have a natter. I'm very partial to the currant bread that my husband bakes. Oh yes, I didn't tell you. My husband's a baker and we did very well during the war, what with the Yanks being over and stationed at Sealand. But I'm so hungry at the moment, any food will do me. I bet you've got a cook and a scullery maid, Ingrid and someone to polish your shoes— Ahhhhh!"

She found herself flying down the stairs, with the wooden floor ahead looming up to meet her and with a thud the world went black for Rita Atkinson, until she saw in the distance a bright and shining light. The house became eerily silent and Ingrid, feeling stunned, watched the scene from the landing, whilst her mind refused to think.

Alerted by the sudden trilling of the telephone, she carefully walked down the stairs towards the body, which seemed to be lying at a sort of twisted angle. Taking no notice of the telephone, in case it was somebody wanting to know her whereabouts, she felt for a pulse in her mother's neck, something she had seen Frank do once when their labrador had died.

Then running swiftly into the dining room, not pausing to register that the daily woman had forgotten to remove some of the breakfast things from underneath it, she grabbed the wooden hostess trolley and with its wheels squeaking in protest, as it had never before been pushed so quickly, she brought it to a halt in the hallway.

Hauling the body across the vehicle, an easy thing to do as Rita was a lightweight, she dashed along the corridor to the kitchen and out through the door to the orangery. It was a pleasant place similar to a conservatory, with a grapevine trailing overhead and a couple of exotic plants in terracotta pots and Ingrid spent many an afternoon there chatting with her friends.

Here, with her way forward becoming a little more difficult because the wicker chairs and their bright red cushions, along with the neat little table and the plaited mats, were inhibiting a smooth passage for the laden hostess trolley and when she looked back, she saw that a couple of pieces of broken crockery had fallen onto the tiled kitchen floor, she had to think quickly about what she was going to do.

So grabbing her mother's lifeless body into her arms, which had now become heavier as rigor mortis had begun to set in, Ingrid stumbled through the open door and down the cobbled path. As she made her way unsteadily through the garden, where herbs and vegetables grew in much profusion, feeling thankful that she was as fit as a flea because of her youth, her weekly game of tennis and all the walks she took through the nearby forest, her hands beginning to feel the weight of her burden, were becoming numb with every step she took. She just managed to let herself out of the wooden gate, where she began to move with increasing difficulty along the sodden muddy track.

It wasn't far before she found a suitable place to dump her onerous load. A place that would be well hidden amongst the tall ferns, grassy undergrowth and behind a rowan tree, whose branches were laden with tiny orange berries. There she laid her hated mother down to rest, with as much regard as she would have had, if she was disposing of the contents of her litter bin.

She still had time to meet her friends if she hurried, Ingrid thought, after she had gathered up the pieces of broken crockery and replaced the hostess trolley back against the wall in the dining room, putting the breakfast dishes that hadn't been broken onto a tray to be dealt with later. She'd wash her hands, brush her hair, change her shoes as they were very dirty, then drive her bright and shiny shooting brake into the village. But first she must think of a way to destroy her mother's handbag, with its ration card, compact, lipstick and I.D.

Chapter Ten

In the autumn of 1953, a young man with a large nose, a wide mouth, a long dark beard on his suntanned face and tight curls that he had grown to shoulder length, appeared one morning at the cottage. He was dressed quite well considering that he was a drifter, but perhaps a local housewife in one of the terraced houses in Prenton might have identified the white shirt and the brown corduroy trousers that he was wearing, as items from her washing line. The long black jacket that he wore as well, had been appropriated from the back of a chair in someone else's kitchen, but it wasn't in Jethro Robinson's nature to rob things from other folk, it was done to necessitate his survival. It was needs must, as he had to live by his wits.

Jethro had been born in Liverpool in 1934, the result of a quick coupling between a silly young girl who was looking for love from anyone who would give her some and a seaman from a ship that had anchored in one of the docks, with a hold full of sugar cane. Taken to an orphanage after the girl's parents were horrified to find that their illegitimate grandchild was a half-caste and the mother-and-baby home where he was born had no one waiting to adopt a child with such an inappropriate lineage, Jethro remained in the institution until he was fourteen.

He was given the name of Jethro Robinson. He assumed as he got older that it had been his mother who had made this choice before she was forced to give him away, which was something he had in common with some of the other children who lived in the orphanage. In fact his name was thought up by the matron of the establishment because the mother hadn't even bothered to register the little thing. Matron had named him Robinson, because the child reminded her of the tale of the castaway who had rescued a native from the cannibals and Jethro as she fancied the name was biblical and sounded more exotic.

Life was tough for the small boy who, because of no fault of his own, had a different appearance to the others. At first when he was just a toddler he was cute and cuddly to the nursery staff, especially to a young woman called Dolores who loved him like her own. It was later when he joined the local school, that he found that the world could be a nasty place, when the boys he met in the playground called him horrible names. 'Black bastard' and 'nigger boy' was used by the bullies as a form of torment, although it had come as a surprise to Jethro that he was the recipient of their taunts, as he had never looked in a mirror and assumed he looked the same. It wasn't until another little boy, called Sergio, a child who lived nearby with his poor Italian parents, who joined the class mid-term, that the bullying stopped and the 'Eyetie' became their target.

It all made young Jethro very bitter about his parentage and he was reluctant to trust his peers at the school again. Instead he grew a chip upon his shoulder in his formative years and looked for sneers where there weren't any.

It was a different story in the place he called home, which was an orphanage just off Cambridge Street and managed by the Liverpool Corporation. Under the auspices of social services, it was a tightly run ship ruled by the man in charge, Leonard Cowling, who didn't tolerate bullying of any kind. He was sympathetic to the plight of the children in his charge, but a firm believer in spare the rod and spoil the child. Cleanliness was next to Godliness and he gave them all a daily dose of religion, weekly baths and the Virol supplement which was to ward off chesty colds. The Ten Commandments had to be obeyed or woe betide the wrongdoer, but it was the forgiveness bit that Jethro found difficult to understand in his harsh, unkind world.

Jethro made himself comfortable on the very dirty and smelly bedding that people had used for over half of a century and looking around, thought that the cottage could be home for the next couple of days. It was isolated, just what he wanted after sleeping rough for the last few months in farmer's barns in various parts of the Wirral, or in derelict outhouses and under the country hedgerows of Storeton in the summer. There was the constant threat of being spotted by someone in authority and beng sent to serve in a foreign place, where he didn't want to go.

Being surrounded by many trees, some that looked quite ancient, the cottage could be just the place to settle for a time. He had money, earned on the streets of Birkenhead, where he had sat on the pavement for many hours holding out a begging hand, and he had visited Elm Stores, the shop in the nearby village earlier and had bought a small block of cheese and a pack of butter for a meal. He had purchased a bloomer from the bakery and treated himself to a succulent looking pie and he thought that he might even try his hand at milking the cows he had seen in a nearby field.

It had been the lads he had worked with at the metal box factory that had put him wise to the fact, that as soon as you were eighteen you were liable for conscription and could be sent abroad. He had gone to work at the factory at fourteen and was told he would be trained to become a presser there. Not that he had ever achieved such an elevated position, as for the past four years his job had been to sweep up the scraps of waste metal from the floor in the press shop and load it into the bins that were transported in a lorry to the railway sidings.

Home now was a room he shared with two others in a local hostel. It didn't bother him that he still had to share; he had been used to sharing in the orphanage dormitory and had no aspirations of having a place of his own. Though somewhere in the back of his mind, he thought that he might meet a girl one day and marry her, but that was in the future.

Upon leaving the orphanage which had been his home for all those years, Jethro, tall for his age and slender, had been given a suit, a change of underwear, a black overcoat, two pairs of socks, and a pair of lace-up shoes. He would have liked the opportunity to emigrate to Australia, as after the war many of the children from the orphanage had been sent there. He thought he might have got a job as a labourer in one of the factories, as he had heard that the country needed to replace the men who had died supporting the British Forces. Unfortunately, Jethro because of his colour, wasn't encouraged to apply.

Dolores, the woman who still worked at the orphanage and now had the older children in her care, had suggested that he lodge with her whilst he looked about for somewhere else to live, near his place of work. But although Jethro loved Dolores like a mother, he didn't want a daily reminder of where he'd come from, nor did he have a desire to look for any family as some of the other orphans had done. He assumed that his mother had left him to his fate, to be brought up by strangers, just because of the colour of his skin; if he had been a white boy she would have kept him and not been ashamed of him.

He was a loner and when he'd finished his training as a presser, like the company had promised that he would do one day, he planned to see the world beyond Liverpool as a man with a much needed skill. Perhaps he could work in one of the newly opened car factories that he had heard about down in the Midlands, or work over the water at Cammel Lairds making ships.

At that time, he hadn't known that seeing the world beyond the city of his birth would mean being trapped in the army for a couple of years. It wasn't until a fellow worker in the press room received his summons from the National Service that Jethro even knew. It appeared from listening later to a debate over brew time, that you were only allowed to side-skip serving if you were an apprentice or went to university. Though if you had wealthy parents who could pay for a solicitor to argue your case for non-conscription, then you didn't have to go.

The young men from ordinary backgrounds, like they were at the factory, had only the choice of disappearing from the face of the earth or they bit the bullet and got on with it. It was said that joining the army or the air force was the makings of a young man, but Jethro knew with certainty, that because of the colour of his skin he would become a target. The bullying would start again, from men this time, not boys that he at least had a chance to fight back with, or even someone in authority who had a down on a coloured man.

Jethro smirked, as he thought of the way he had got away with being conscripted. He had never been given that coveted apprenticeship, which would have guaranteed a deferral from National Service. He still got used as a labourer after working at the company for over for four years. So as soon as he could, he had gone into a pawnshop and bought an old kit bag for carrying his things. He swapped his suit for more suitable, durable clothing, as that month it had snowed and there were bitter temperatures. In exchange for his suit, he got a thick knitted Guernsey jumper, two pairs of ancient looking corduroys and a woolly hat that covered his tied back hair. It was a different-looking young man who stared into the pawnshop's cheval mirror, a strange-looking being even to himself. No one would know where Jethro Robinson had gone, once he had left his accommodation and jacked in his job. He assumed a limp, a bad one, which involved a walking stick to help him along and most people didn't look at the face of a beggar, who was sitting on the pavement outside one of the shops in Grange Road which had an awning, just the pennies they were dropping into his tin.

Nora began to see a light amongst the murkiness every time the voices were around. She began to see her death with utmost clarity, something she had never seen before. She could hear the sound of her little boy's screams and see the jagged tear on the side of her brow from when she had struck her head on the corner of the hearth. As she lay amongst the fallen blackberries on the stone-flagged floor, she saw that her husband was hunkered down beside her, rubbing her arms, shouting her name, trying to bring her back from the brink of the death where she found herself teetering. She saw her grave which he had dug in the orchard under one of the apple trees, then heard the voices in the distance calling her name. The voice she could hear the loudest was the sweetest of them all. It was her boy, her lovely boy who was now in the spirit world. The light at the end of the tunnel was its brightest and she could sense the pull to hold him, as she had when he lived on the earth.

The fair-haired girl, who stood at the door of the cottage a few days after Jethro took up residence, stared curiously through into the kitchen as she saw that the place was occupied once more. Beggarman's Cottage and its grounds was a haven for the seven-year-old. It was the place where she took sanctuary from her angry parents next door.

Alison Sheldon, the elder daughter of the occupants of Redstone House, was surprised to see this bearded young man, with his head full of tight curls that reminded her of the black doll with the colourful turban, that she had been given as a Christmas present last year. At first glance as she peeped through the door, Alison thought that the figure must be Pete. The kindly old man who always put his arms around her and gave her a hug if she happened across him. He was usually there to sleep off one of his boozy treks to see his mates, who lived under the trestle tables in Birkenhead Market.

She had been just about to say 'Boo' to the fellow, hoping to give him a fright as she usually tried to do, when she saw Jethro. She gazed boldly at him, when he turned from where he was making himself a cheese sandwich on top of one of the window bottoms and noticed that she was standing there.

"Want some?" he asked cautiously, proffering half of the sandwich in her direction and was quite surprised to hear that she sounded quite confident in her reply. Most little children ran away from Jethro if they ever came across him in the street.

"No, thank you, I've just eaten. Mother made us some soup for our lunch. Are you staying here overnight as my friend Pete does? Only he might not be happy if he finds you here, nor will my father be neither."

"Oh. I didn't know the place belonged to anyone, I thought with the door being on its hinges and the place in a bit of a mess that anyone was allowed to live here." He made his voice sound as if he was joking, he didn't want her running away and alerting someone in authority.

"The cottage belongs to my father, but he says it's a bloody liability… whoops, pardon my French, will you."

Jethro smiled. She was a cute little thing, dressed as she was in a navy blue knee-length dress, a thick dark blue knitted cardigan, long white socks and black lace-up shoes and now she was blushing after parroting her parent.

"Do come in," he said in a posh accent, something he had heard from listening to the accent of the wife of the man who owned the metal box company. He swished his arm towards her as if he was inviting royalty into a smart residence and she smiled at his humour and wandered in.

"Are you sure that Madam wouldn't like to share my sandwich?" he asked, making himself comfortable on the makeshift bed, after stowing the loaf of bread, pack of butter, block of cheese and his penknife in his kit bag.

"My name's Alison, not Madam," she giggled. "I'm seven years old and I go to the County Primary School. I don't like it there though, all the teachers shout and the headmaster has a stick that he hits the boys with and I sit next to a boy who smells of wee wee."

"Sounds like the school I used to go to," Jethro said sympathetically.

"Oh, did you go to school?" Alison sounded amazed for some reason.

"Everyone has to go to school, even your parents would have gone some time."

"Oh. Did *you* used to have horrid teachers and a horrid headmaster then and a boy who smelt of wee wee?"

"It was more that the other children at school were horrid to me, but not the teachers," Jethro said sadly, whilst thinking that most of the boys from the back streets of Liverpool smelt awful, much as he did now.

"Oh, there's this one boy in my class who's a real bully. I hate him," said Alison in a matter of fact voice, who by this time had made herself comfortable on top of another bundle of rags that she had moved to sit near him. She was warming to this man, who looked a bit different from the people she had seen before during her tender years, but if you weren't frightened because of his beard, he was nice to talk to.

"His name is Roy Froggatt and he's always getting me into trouble with the teacher. He's a snitch and he likes to give you Chinese burns."

"Have you told your parents?"

How much easier would his life have been, had *he* been able to talk his troubles over with a parent, although motherly Dolores had listened to his woes when he lived in the orphanage.

"No, Father would go mad and probably kill him. I don't tell my father anything and I don't hate Roy *that* much that I would want him killed. Anyway, how long are you staying here?"

"Until my money runs out. I'll have to move on in a couple of days."

"Oh money, "The root of all evil," my mother says. Where do you think you'll go to? My friend Pete lives in a place called Neston. He has a boat now and he says you can live off fish if you want to, so you don't have to have money. Anyway, I suppose I'd better go. I don't want Mother coming to look for me or she'll know you are here and tell Father. I don't want him to kill you, as you look a nice person. Perhaps tomorrow when I come to see you, you might like me to make you happy."

"Happy?"

"You know, Pete likes me to play with his willy, he says it makes him happy. I could play with yours if you want me to. Toodle-oo."

Jethro watched in alarm as the little girl skipped her way out of the cottage and into the orchard. He jumped to his feet. He was going to have to get out of there as quick as he could, even if it meant walking through the night to somewhere.

He knew all about the lost innocence of youth and what it could do to the naivety of your childhood. Jethro had lost his innocence, when five inquisitive lads had dragged him into the boy's toilets at playtime, to see if his black features extended to his private place. He'd been ten at the time, on the verge of his puberty and ignorant in his belief that what he called his 'jimmy' was only used for weeing through. He didn't understand their jibes about his manhood, nor understand why he'd been singled out that day, as they usually confined their bullying to taunts about his parentage. But this particular playtime there was an older boy, who had been using the urinals when the lads had dragged poor Jethro in and he had taken the opportunity to humiliate him.

He still had nightmares, if sometimes his mind began to wander back to that horrible time in his childhood, but he usually managed to deal with them, but not today. Someone should tell her mother or the authorities what was happening to that poor little girl, but Jethro decided, rightly or wrongly, it wasn't going to be him.

Chapter Eleven

Jethro made his way along the Arrowe Brook Lane, listening to an owl who was hooting in the branches of a tree nearby and the scurrying of little nocturnal animals as they went on their search for food. The harvest moon shone brightly in a multitude of twinkling stars, as the night was cold and it would probably be frosty in the morning.

He knew he could find shelter in one of the outbuildings that stood near a farmhouse and there was also a Dutch barn. He had stayed in there on a couple of previous occasions. In fact one time he had thrown caution to the wind and helped bring in the harvest, loading the bales of hay onto the lorries that came up from Birkenhead. Having been rewarded with a good meal, courtesy of the housekeeper who lived at the farm, and allowed to stay for a short time there, as the weather had turned from calm skies to blustery showers, he reckoned he could hole up there for a few days without any worries.

He wandered into the cobbled stack-yard, listening to the pigs as they grunted quietly in their pens and the hens who clucked nervously in their wooden coops as the sound of his heavy working man's boots resounded on the stones. Then once around the rear of the house where the privy was housed in the orchard, Jethro decided that he would move his bowels in comfort, rather than having to go behind a hedge like he usually did.

All was quiet there, the occupants must have been abed and the black dog, who he remembered used to be tied up near the

Dutch barn, must have been taken indoors. He sat astride the privy, relishing this bit of comfort that didn't often occur, when suddenly he heard a snarling outside the privy door. He realised in a panic that it was the dog, probably been let loose and allowed to wander. He froze, then his heart started hammering as the door was pushed open and a male voice commanded the dog to attack.

Jethro's knees and calfs were bare, as he had pushed his trousers down to his ankles and he shrieked in agony as sharp fangs bit deeply. And as he passed out from the pain, he banged his head on the sandstone wall.

He awoke to find a pair of brown eyes looking anxiously down upon him and for a split second it occurred to him that the woman's face might belong to his mother, as there was concern in those dark-skinned features as she held his hand. Then the moment passed, as he realised that the person standing beside the bed was dressed in a uniform and why would the woman who had given birth to him nearly twenty years ago, be suddenly concerned about his welfare?

"You've awoken at last," said Nurse Gabriel in her Caribbean lilt whilst looking relieved as she lifted Jethro's head and pushed a cup of water to his lips. "We thought you were a gonner. You've been lying in a coma for the last couple of days."

"Where am I?" Jethro asked, trying to pull himself up, but the effort of doing so caused his head to pound, as if there were a hundred hammers knocking. And the pain in his right leg was horrendous, he had never felt so much pain before! He sank back onto the pillow with a moan and the nurse went to fetch the ward sister.

"You are in St. Catherine's Hospital after giving yourself a nasty knock," the sister said, making him more comfortable by putting another pillow behind him, so that he could sit up. "You were brought here on the back of a farm cart which didn't help matters, though it probably accounted for the terrible smell. I have given you an injection and to ward off possible infection we have had the wound cauterised, then Doctor stitched the skin together and now you should be as right as rain. And although you were brought in concussed, you appear to have recovered, so rest and some medication will do the trick. However, now that you're awake, I believe I have to contact the Birkenhead police to take a statement from you."

Jethro felt petrified. Not only had he been nearly mauled to death by a dog and ended up in hospital, he could well end up in prison for running away as well. He'd have to slip away as soon as he was left alone, but for the next couple of hours there was no chance, as pretty Nurse Gabriel in her green dress and white pinafore, always seemed to be hanging around.

First there had been a bed bath, tenderly given with avoidance of the large bandage that now encased his leg, after being put into a pair of standard hospital pyjamas which didn't quite fit across his chest. Then along came a policeman, who sat at the side of his bed.

Constable Uttley, a stern-looking individual in his forties, took out a pencil and a notebook from the breast pocket of his uniform. This was the man lying in the hospital bed who, it had been reported, had been bitten badly by a farm dog. According to the matron whom he had just been talking to Mr. Robinson had been brought in concussed as well. It was time to get his side of the story.

"Name and address first, sir," he said, looking at the young man who was clearly from one of the commonwealth countries, judging by his tight black hair and suntanned features.

"My name is Jethro Robinson and I don't have a place to live at the moment."

"Ah, not from one of our commonwealth countries then, sir, but you look too young to have fought in the war."

"No, I didn't. I mean, yes I am too young to have fought in the war and I'm from Liverpool." He could feel his voice wobbling, as he could see where the questioning from the policeman was leading.

"Ah, so you'll be due to be called up for the National Service then, sir. Especially as of being of no fixed abode you could be run in for vagrancy. But first we'll have to get you well again and then you can report to the police station on Borough Road when you're discharged from here."

"But what about the dog, shouldn't he be shot for causing my injuries? I mean he took a bite out of my leg and caused me to bang my head on the privy wall."

"Only doing his job, sir. According to the farmer, who gave us a statement after he brought you in, you shouldn't have been on his property in the first place and that is why he set his dog upon you." Constable Uttley closed his notebook and prepared to leave the ward.

"Don't forget, report to the station as soon as you get the all-clear and don't be foolish enough to think you can make a run for it. Not with a poorly leg."

Jethro was left to contemplate his doom as a soldier in the British Army.

It was the following morning and Nurse Gabriel, who had stayed behind at the end of her shift the day before because she was so concerned about the fate of her patient. After she had listened to the young man's fears of being put into the British Army, she came quietly to Jethro's bed and asked him how he was feeling that day. It was her duty to be concerned about her patients, she had told herself, as she lay in her bed at the Nurse's Home earlier and thought of the day ahead, whilst looking forward to seeing Mr. Robinson. She was a young Christian woman, aged twenty-two, from Jamaica, who had come over from her homeland to help fill the nursing shortage caused by the war and was feeling lonely.

After being shaved of the ridiculously long beard and having had a bit of a haircut and smelling better because of the bed bath she had given him, Mr. Robinson was quite good looking, she thought. She would pray that his wound would heal quickly and perhaps if she prayed hard enough, she could come up with a solution regarding his future.

For some reason, Nurse Gabriel felt rather drawn to him. Whether it was because of his dark features, when everyone around her was white-skinned, she wasn't sure, but he had told her that, before he had been bitten by the farm dog, he'd been living rough in the countryside. It was her aim to help him and later that day felt as if her prayers had been answered, when there on the notice board was a card advertising for a hospital porter.

What a miracle that would be. She could see Mr. Robinson every day if he was given the job as a porter and if he was excused from the army on medical grounds, because of the wound in his leg, who knew what the future could hold for herself and Jethro.

In 1969, when the world was becoming a very different place to the one that Nora might have known if she had lived past her twenty-first birthday, Alison's father was toying with the idea of demolishing the dilapidated cottage next door. With the roof that now leaked, which was causing black mould to grow up the inner walls; the chimney that had now begun to lurch to one side drunkenly; and the cost of replacing the doors and windows that were regularly staved-in by would-be inhabitants, the place had become an eyesore.

It was also rage that had brought on this fit of pique against the old building in the end. Firstly because Alison and her husband Graham with their two boys, Connor and 'Band Aid' baby Nathan, had emigrated to Australia a couple of months before. It was much to Catherine's dismay and Geoffrey's loosening of power over the decisions of his family, but also because in a moment lacking in sensibility when Geoffrey was considering the cottage's demolition, Catherine had confided that she would also be happy to see it razed to the ground, because of the unhappy memories it held.

He hadn't really listened to what his wife had said at that time, being so incensed to be losing a daughter and his grandchildren to a country on the other side of the world, whilst his younger daughter, Linda, had no inclination towards providing his grandsons' replacements, as she hadn't even got a ring on her finger. Nearly twenty years old and more interested in riding horses from the stables at Thurstaston, than looking for a man. And Alison, well if that's what she wanted to do with life, than so be it. She should never have married that no good Graham Mason in the first place.

The way things were going, there was no point in having a business to hand down to his descendants, so he may as well put his feet up. All that work that he had done since he'd been handed part of the company on a silver plate by his great uncle, Michael, the employment he had brought to the locals, the quality of workmanship that he had insisted upon whilst raising the avenues of middle-class villas after the war, had been a waste of time. Although he had to admit that it was because of being given the company on a silver plate in the first place, that he had managed exemption from conscription. He and his workforce had been in great demand, shoring up the bomb damage inflicted by over sixty raids on Birkenhead and Liverpool.

Selling the grounds that the cottage stood on and they were quite substantial, enough for a farmer to be interested in grazing his herd of sheep upon it, or a market gardener who could be gainfully employed selling his produce to the masses, who still visited the area to enjoy the sea air. It could also be that someone might consider opening up a garden centre. Many people liked to get their hands dirty in their gardens nowadays.

Whatever happened, the sale of the land would provide Catherine and himself with a life of ease as they neared the age of retirement. Perhaps a journey abroad to seek a little sun in the winter, though not Australia because of all the travelling, or he could even purchase a villa in Spain. Somewhere in a warmer climate where they could escape from the interminable freezing winters. There would be endless possibilities once he had done the deed. Although Catherine, as she had grown older, had become a bit of a home bird and it was even difficult to get her to agree to a run out to Llandudno.

This particular evening, after they had enjoyed a homemade steak and kidney pie, the pastry being Catherine's speciality, along with a strawberry trifle she had made, Geoff decided to bring the subject up, as her words had niggled him all day. What had she meant when she said that the cottage had brought her unhappy memories? He wasn't aware that she had even set foot inside the place, since they had moved into Redstone House all those years ago.

"It was when Alison left Graham and stayed the night there," she said, thinking that what she was about to tell him was so far back in time, it had been silly to have even mentioned it. She had always kept away from what the locals called 'Beggarman's Cottage' for that very reason, because she might stumble across a beggar who was sleeping rough.

Besides, the place had an eery feel about it, as if someone had been watching them from the kitchen window, when they had stood there in the orchard on their wedding day. She knew about these things, because her father had been a spiritualist and had always been able to feel any ghostly vibes around him.

"I didn't tell you at the time because you and Graham were having a bit of an altercation in the lane and when Alison appeared from the cottage, you were so angry that she had stayed there instead of with us, that I let the subject go. But do you remember, many years ago, that there was that hobo who used to stop at the cottage on his way back from visiting his friends at the Birkenhead market? I'm talking when Alison was about seven?" She took a deep breath before she continued. "Well, out of the blue, she told me that when she used to play in the cottage and that tramp was there, things went on that I don't want to elaborate upon. Geoffrey, you know, I think I'm talking about... his thing down below. I hadn't realised she was in such danger, but she was never one to confide in people. She was always so secretive when she was a child."

Her hands shook suddenly, as she stood by the draining board drying the clean plates with a tea towel. *Why did I just come out with it like that?* she chastised herself, as she turned to take a look at her husband. She should never have said anything at all. Geoffrey had gone red in the face and looked as if he was about to have a heart attack!

"It was a long time ago, darling. I think she only said it because she was trying to justify why she wanted to leave her husband at that time. I know she found it incredibly hard to speak to me with it being such a personal subject, but I think she might have been trying to tell me why she had such a distaste of their marital relationship. It was only when she grew older and realised that the old man was just a horrible pervert taking advantage of her trusting nature, that she examined her feelings towards the males in her life."

"What do you mean, 'she examined her feelings towards the males in her life?'" Geoffrey roared! "Damn it, Catherine, what are you saying? I knew she was promiscuous, but how many other men has she been with that I don't know about?"

"Geoffrey, calm down, I'm only repeating what she told me in confidence and as far as I know there have only ever been three young men in her life." Catherine was aghast that she had let slip to her very volatile husband what Alison had told her and watched in disbelief as he went to the back of one of the kitchen chairs to get his coat.

"What are you doing? Old Pete will have died long ago. He must have been seventy when he used to pass this way. He's not been seen for years."

"Ah, but I can prevent it happening again with some other kiddie fiddler. I'm going to the shed to get a lump hammer. I've wanted to get rid of that bloody place for a long time, as you know. It's just a shelter now for down and outs and vagabonds. It'll never be a family home again. I'll make a start myself and bring Gary and Jed around in the morning. They can earn their bloody wages for once."

It was around this time that Nora began to have a feeling that she had never experienced. The familiar voices from her family had stopped calling and there was a strange silence, except for the hooting of an owl outside. Then from her position near the hearth she began to hear the sound of crashing, perhaps another wounded soul was trying to gain access through the cottage's front door. When the door began to splinter and then there was the sound of shattering glass, Nora retreated to the orchard and watched as a man began to swing his hammer through the already broken kitchen windowpanes. He then stood gasping whilst he got his breath.

She felt her spirit being pulled in different directions. Firstly towards the big old oak tree where Rosemary had hidden in those boughs so many years ago, then towards Nora's shallow grave under one of the apple trees, where Walter had buried her body after he had struck her that day. Finally back in the direction of her dwelling place, where the man had come and was demolishing her earthly attachment: the place where many people had found sanctuary from whatever plight they had found themselves in.

She had been there for every one of them. She had created a calming presence for the men who had ran away in fear from what might have been done to them if they hadn't: Jack, the conscientious objector; Joseph, the German Jew; Jethro, the orphan boy; and Christopher, who had fled from his stepfather. Also the young girls, Ingrid and Olga. Ingrid, a grown woman with a damning secret that could bring possible disruption to her happy life and Alison, the daughter of this man who was wielding a hammer forcefully and who appeared to have gone a little mad. Not to mention the horrible hobo, who had done that deed which Nora shuddered to even think about. If there was a hell somewhere, she hoped he was in it, roasting his appendage in the fires within.

Then there was her own dear boy whom she had managed to see grown up as a man. One day she would be reunited with her Thomas, wherever that would be.

The deed was done and Nora watched as lorry after lorry load of rubble was driven away. The chimney breast and the hearth came last, then Geoffrey's workmen busied themselves clearing up the broken glass, the slates from the roof and the cottage floor, chimney pots and the fire grate. All the debris that had amassed within Beggarman's Cottage over the last century, was trundled away in sturdy, mortar-flecked wheelbarrows, with the men nodding wearily as they listened to Geoffrey shout.

Chapter Twelve

It had been a long and weary journey, starting three whole days before, when the Mason family had set off from Lime Street Station in Liverpool, to travel by train to Gatwick. It had been snowing in Britain as they took off from the airport and much later, after thirty-five hours of sitting on a Trans-Australia plane, would eventually land in Sydney on Australia's east coast; they were all hoping that they would soon be feeling the warmth of the sun on their faces. There had been few stops on their journey. Only for the plane to refuel and food brought on to feed the passengers, who were mostly 'Ten Pound Poms' looking for a better life. Many of these people, who had sat in cramped conditions onboard the Boeing 727, could have been forgiven if they wondered if the journey had been worth it.

It was January 1969, and Alison and Graham Mason were amongst those passengers, who boarded the plane from London to Sydney. Along with their two children, Connor and Nathan, they would later catch a domestic flight from Sydney to Adelaide, where Graham was to work in place called Elizabeth. The town was named after Queen Elizabeth who had visited the area in 1963.

Tempted by the notices for workers to help build a new Australia, which seemed to pop up in the local newspaper on a regular basis, Graham who was used to driving Daimler buses with a conductor on the platform at the back, had been told that in the future he would be driving the new Atlantean buses and would be taking the fares as well.

In a fit of pique, or more probably nervous about coping with money as well because he wasn't very good at arithmetic, he had decided that he would rather work on the other side of the world instead.

Besides taking his boys away from the unpredictable weather and the high-rise flat on the council estate, the prospects in a new country would be boundless. There would be better education for the children, better work prospects for him and they might even be able to afford a house one day with a swimming pool!

Alison had gone along with his plans and dreams after he had contacted Australia House in London. She had no option if she still wanted to be part of her children's lives, as she knew that he would fight her in court for the custody of them.

Graham, after that first flush of joy when his errant wife had come dashing out of Beggarman's Cottage, had returned to his bullying ways. She still had to hide from the tally woman when Graham had his latest 'must have' on hire purchase and she was not allowed a say in anything anymore. Nancy, his mother, had been cross that Alison had returned, even if her daughter-in-law had her tail between her legs, as she had envisaged a cosy haven for herself, with just her son and little Connor and regular weekly housekeeping and she had rubbed in the facts of Alison's return at every opportunity.

Alison, with plenty of her time on her hands on that hated flight to their new life, crammed as she was in a window seat, where now and again she would glimpse the vastness of the barren Australian landscape below, was unable to sleep except for the occasional nod and reflected on her situation whilst her children lay sleeping.

It had been obvious that Nancy had not expected Graham to talk his wife into returning. The woman had already brought over her suitcase and Alison discovered later, that her few clothes had been hung in the small wardrobe in Connor's room. The child had been crying when she and Graham got home. Evidence of his tears still showing on his cheeks, as his Nana prepared to put him in his highchair.

"So Graham persuaded yer to come back then," Nancy had said sneeringly, clutching onto her grandchild, as he stretched out his arms for his mother to take him. "More fool him, is what I say. We were getting on very well without yer."

"Leave it, Mother, she knows what side her bread's buttered. She knows I'd get custody of Connor if it were to go to court. Get yer coat off, Ali', and feed our Connor. I'll run Mum back home."

Alison had said nothing, she was a bit in shock if the truth was told. One minute she was thinking about making a new life for herself, albeit without her boy until she could go to court and try to claim custody herself and the next minute she was back in Graham's clutches and virtually a prisoner in the two room flat. Was this it, another forty years or so of being married to Graham Mason? If it hadn't been for Connor, she would have considered taking an overdose, though it had only been a fleeting thought. She would have to stay with her husband until Connor was a lot older, but when she got to thirty-nine there would be still time to get a career. And perhaps in the future, Graham would allow her to study at night school.

Fat chance of that, she mused, staring bitterly at her sleeping husband who had his mouth slightly open as he snored, who had made himself comfortable across a couple of seats in front that hadn't been occupied, he had almost dragged her to the bedroom after Connor had been laid down for his afternoon nap. Flinging her down onto the bed he had in essence raped her, though being a married couple she had no recourse over that. Pushing up her skirt and ripping at her panties, as she tried in vain to stop his onslaught, he had pinned her down with one hand, then after pushing her legs apart with the other, he had lunged his bulging penis into her body, not caring that she protested wildly at his assault upon her, as she thrashed herself around.

Her resistance seemed to excite him even further because within seconds he had discharged his load and lay panting beside her, whilst she lay passive, hating every fibre of his being. To add insult to injury he had left her with a love bite on her neck, which she was loathe to have on show for her mother-in-law, who was quite likely to make a coarse remark about their coupling. And she didn't dare visit her mother for at least two weeks, as Catherine would have been horrified.

Nine months later, she had given birth to little Nathan, though she had to admit he was such a little treasure. He was worth every minute of the life she had put on hold to be a mother to him and Connor, she thought, looking down with love at the toddler who slept beside her. Both he and Connor, a serious little boy of three years old were her world now and she would do the best she could for both of them.

Her spirit had gone. Her earthly attachment had been broken. Nora was on the brink of the spirit world, a fuzzy place where shadows of her loved ones waited to welcome her. She felt their presence more than saw who was present and communication was a knowledge, not the spoken word. There was Thomas, reunited with her family, her mother, father and siblings, who stood waiting and Rosemary, her little friend who had died in childbirth when she had married her step-cousin, John Cornelius, and was waiting to greet her.

She knew her son's story now. Returning to his homeland and frightened of being caught up in the hostilities in Dublin and the armed insurrection of those who wanted freedom from British rule, he had escaped to live in Sligo, a bustling seaport on the northwest shores. In the town, not too far away from his kith and kin, he had worked for a small business and had switched to designing ships for the new company. He had married, his wife had bore a son and Thomas would still be living with his family to a ripe old age, if it hadn't been for the outbreak of the Second World War. One day, aboard a ship that hadn't had its maiden voyage and was being put through its paces by the designers before its launch, it had sank in the middle of the Atlantic Ocean and to that day the cause was still unknown.

Time has no meaning in the spirit world and many disembodied souls appeared to float around in perpetuity. There was a sense of waiting for a happening, an occurrence for the occupants of the gloom. Though if you happened across a spirit that bore an association with your earthly life, a vague fuzzy brightness that had no formation, would appear.

A disembodied soul who manifested his presence to Nora was Joseph Inkerman and he told his tale of hardship in a foreign land.

On the arrival of the Dunera in Sydney that following September, the skeletal bodies of the alien passengers were rounded up and transported through the night on a train, which was bound for an internment camp in New South Wales. Their treatment by the Australian guards was in stark contrast to the British guards, as they were given food, fruit and cigarettes during their travels and treated kindly.

They were interned for a while in three high-security camps near a town called Hay, chosen for its isolation and temperate climate. The conditions there were not so bad, and many of the interns were ingenious men who put together a soccer team or entertained the others with concerts.

But in 1941 when the Japanese bombed Pearl Harbor, the passengers from the Dunera, who lived in camps seven and eight and were deemed to be no threat to anyone, were re-classified as *friendly aliens* by the Australian government and released.

Some of these people chose to join the Australian army, some were offered residency and many went back to Britain to take up their lives again. Joseph was one of those released from the camp who chose to become a resident, feeling resentful that the British government had treated him and his fellow aliens in the way that they had and had no wish to return to a country, which was still at risk of attack from the German planes.

He had sent a letter from the Hay Military Post Office to Dorothy, asking her to join him in Australia where together they could start a new life. To the day of his demise, he had never known if she had received his invitation, because she never replied and he was yet to find her or his family in the spirit world.

He was given the choice of settling in Tatura in the Goulburn Valley, where there was a need for workers in the dairy farming industry or Orange in New South Wales. Joseph chose Orange, as although it was a fruit-growing area that mainly grew apples and pears, it also had a small open-cut gold mine. Attracted by the thought of finding gold and returning to Dorothy as a wealthy man, he was given a travel permit and caught the train to Bourke where he intended to begin his search.

"I had set off to walk with another man, who had been with me since we started our Australian journey. Samuel, a fellow German, had lost track of his wife after the Nazi's herded the Jews into the Berlin ghettos. He had left our homeland to work in Liverpool, because the depression at that time in Germany meant there was little work to be had, especially if you were Jew. When war was declared, Samuel was one of the first to be interned as an alien.

"There were many miles to walk before we reached our destination. Hungry, thirsty and very tired, we took shelter in one of the orchards on our way and feasted on a glut of pears that had fallen on the ground. Windfalls, I think you call them, but an hour or so later, Samuel and I pitched up the contents of our stomachs and we virtually crawled through the orchard, where a kindly woman took us into her farmhouse.

"Weakened and dehydrated, we were in no fit state then to work in a gold mine, where labouring there could have caused our early demise, but with Australia still sending troops abroad and the threat of a Japanese attack on the north of the country, men were few and the farmer gave us jobs picking fruit in his orchards.

"But I still kept thinking of wondrous riches and becoming stronger. It wasn't long before I bought a gold pan, a shovel, a pick and a tin pannikin. I had heard that there were gold-bearing sands and gravel in the Macquarie River and abandoned workings, where it was possible to find an ounce of gold each day. I set off alone one

morning, although Samuel had implored me not to leave as he thought
me foolish, but I had this great need in my soul to see my Dorothy
again. The only way I knew was to find a lump of gold to bring me
wealth beyond my dreams and I could travel back to England to find
her. But all that glitters isn't gold and my health broke down in this
pursuit of riches and I died a pauper, a broken man."

It was a few weeks later, after Beggarman's Cottage had been demolished, that a bright red open-top sports car, driven by a fair-haired, well-dressed young man, came to an abrupt stop as the vehicle swerved onto the grassy verge in front of where the building used to be. Climbing quickly out of the vehicle, he looked in disbelief at what he saw. Just the orchard lay within a stone perimeter wall now and the line of oaks and bushes, that had grown to great heights over the years and which had concealed the tumbledown cottage.

Feeling bewildered as to why the cottage had been demolished, he wandered across the overgrown site to where he had taken refuge not so many years before. The young man was Christopher, who now lived with his grandparents in Caldy and had just completed his final term at the local grammar school.

His grandparents, who had given him the sports car for his eighteenth birthday, had given him stability in his teenage years and he had always felt an affinity with the dilapidated old place, when he passed it by on his way to somewhere. There was a connection with the cottage, since as a troubled boy he had sought shelter within its walls. Having had a stepfather foisted upon him, whilst suffering confusion as to why his father had gone away, hadn't boded well at that time in the young man's life, but all that was in the past now. He had been allowed to move into the rather splendid Georgian house, which his grandparents owned, and with his interest in anything historical, especially houses, Christopher hoped that one day when he had finished university, he would be able to visit the architectural sites of interest around the world.

Chapter Thirteen

COURAGE, PRIDE, DREAMS, ACHIEVEMENT
Single men and woman in hundreds of occupations and married
tradesmen are offered assisted passages to Australia. Assured
Employment. Pre-arranged accommodation. Pre-paid flights.

That poster had been the lure that helped make Graham Mason's decision to take his family to the other side of the world. As had many others, Alison found, when after being greeted by immigration officials at Adelaide Airport after a four-hour flight from Sydney, forty-six adults and children waited for two buses that would take them north to a place called Elizabeth.

It was hot on that day in January and Alison felt prickles of heat creeping over her body. She wore a summer shirtwaist dress, a plain green one with a wide white belt, and as she hadn't brought a hat, her head felt as if it was about to begin a headache.

Her children though were suitably dressed for this new climate, which they were all going to have to get used to. Catherine, in a moment of anguish the summer before, when she had realised that her grandchildren were to become a fond memory, had given Alison two ten-pound notes and told her to kit the poor boys out. Lightweight clothes, besides the shorts and tops they wore, lay in one of the suitcases, in sizes that would last them a couple of years.

Along the way, Alison had made friends with a girl called Evelyn Dwyer, ("Call me Evie," she was told). Her and husband Tim, a fair-haired chap with a receding hairline, had two boys,

Joe and little Phil, who were roughly the same age as Connor and Nathan and they had met whilst waiting in the airport lounge at Sydney.

Meeting Evie, a plump, red-haired girl with a ready smile and dressed in a colourful kaftan-type top and pair of black wide-bottom trousers, appeared from talking to her, had a heart as pure as gold, which made Alison feel a whole lot better. Even if it was just to be able to chat to someone in the same position.

Not that Evie was averse to leaving her family and friends behind in Liverpool, where the couple had lived before. It had been her who had wanted a better life for her family and she couldn't wait to start it.

"You'll love it," Evie had said enthusiastically as they watched their children playing happily on the cork mats on the floor in front of them, free from their confinement in the cabin of the aeroplane and their husbands, sitting with their heads together, discussing their reasons for emigrating to Australia.

"My sister and her Scottish husband came over on the Stratheden in 1963. It was a bit different than in the old days when people travelled in steerage. They came over in style in a four-berth cabin and Ralph got a job in Whyalla, as he was used to building ships on the Clyde. They've got a great life there, with all the English and Scottish social clubs and a couple of football teams. Like us though they had no choice in their accommodation and ended up in a hostel at first. A bit different, or so Brenda, that's my sister, said, compared with the luxury of ten weeks sailing on the cruise ship. They were put in Nissan huts, where everyone lived on top of each other and it caused a lot of rows. And unbeknown to them, they'd come out in the Aussie winter and everyone had been expecting sunshine. It was chilly, but luckily they'd brought with them all the clothes they possessed. I told her, I thought it was always warm in Australia, but she said bugger that, only from December to April in Adelaide. But then they got a nice flat when the S.A. Trust started a building programme and now they live in a rented house on the Eire Peninsula! Now that our Ellie's gone to school, that's her last one, she has three other kids, my sister's got a part-time job helping in the canteen at the school. They've been saving for their own place and now that they've become permanent residents, they can live where they want to. By the sea if they like."

"Will there be sea at Elizabeth?" Alison hoped that there would be. From her parents' house, if she had stood on a grassy hillock, she could see right over the rolling grasslands to the Irish Sea. She wished she was doing just that at the moment, as a longing for her childhood home and her mother suddenly threatened to overwhelm her.

"Yes, but it will be a bit of a way from where we'll be living, but we could have a day out at the beach if we wanted with the kids. I take it we'll be all together at this place near Goodman Road. At least until our fellows start earning money and we can have a look around. Will you be renting?"

"Of course, we had to rent from the council back at home. Graham never earned enough to get a mortgage. And you?"

"Well, we've got a bit saved up, but not enough to have gone on the Nest Egg Scheme. Brenda was telling me that some of the folk who came over could emigrate without sponsorship, that's if you had five hundred pounds to spare. You could get residency in them days straight away. Not like us who have to give it two years. Then if you had one thousand pounds, lucky jossers, you could go on the Migrant House scheme and you'd be guaranteed house ownership within seven days."

"I wish," said Alison, turning away with tears in her eyes. Why the hell had she married Graham Mason? Here she was stuck forever in a foreign land, even if the people here did speak the same language and drive on the left hand side of the road. She was so hot and so tired now that she could sleep on a park bench if there was one and there was still more travelling before she could put herself to bed.

"Come on, love." Evie patted her on the shoulder sympathetically. "It won't be so bad when we've got ourselves sorted. It's a fresh start for both our families and me and you can stick together if you want."

It was an hour later before they reached their accommodation, which was a two-storey block of flats, wood framed with a brick veneer, and which would be their home for the foreseeable future. Set just off Goodman Road, it was a great improvement on the Nissan huts, old wool sheds and the cramped conditions in the hostels that migrants had known before.

The man from immigration who had accompanied them on the bus was a kind man. A bit officious maybe, but he tried to keep the children on the bus amused with a little magic. "Oohs," and "Ahhs," abounded whilst the man bedazzled them, with disappearing mice made from his white handkerchief and the sticky lolly pops that suddenly appeared behind a little one's ear.

After leaving the airport and feeling rather heartened by seeing the Adelaide Hills in the distance, albeit black as the grass had been scorched by a bush fire recently, the coach passed through areas where industry and streets of housing lived in close proximity, as many were employed in the burgeoning economy of postwar Adelaide. There was the Weapons Research Establishment, General Motors Holden, and a company with the name of James Hardie, all needing workers to man their enterprise. But first there were the formalities.

Leaving their husbands at the desk to pay their first week's rent, be given resident cards, a rules and regulations pamphlet and a map to show them how to get to the migrant's meeting the next morning, Alison and Evie gathered up their, by now, very weary toddlers and following a fresh-faced, fair-haired young woman in a navy blue suit, who they were told to call Jenna, went along the walkway to the flats.

"What kind of weather have you left behind in the old country?" Jenna enquired, as the exhausted party struggled along. "I have a brother who's staying in Manchester. He says it's raining cats and dogs most of the time, so you'll be glad to see our sunshine. Though sometimes it gets so hot here in the summer that we stay indoors. We don't even venture to the beach when it's one hundred and ten degrees."

"So how far away is the beach from here then?" Evie asked, puffing slightly now as her youngest was becoming a heavy handful.

"Dependent on the transport really," came the answer. "St. Kilda's or further south at a place called Glenelg, but there are lots of lovely places in between, such as Largs Bay or Semaphore. Sometimes we take a tent and spend the weekend down to Maslin Beach. It's great there, only the beach and a couple of summer huts along the front and hardly anyone. Though my bloke's got a car – it would take ages to get there on public transport."

The ground-floor flat was larger than expected and access was through a beige tiled hallway with rooms leading off. There were sounds of delight from Connor and Evie's eldest, who suddenly sprang to life when they saw that the child of the last tenants had left a box of toys, a large plastic ball and a beat-up old pedal car behind in the living room, which they climbed into from both sides, immediately. The children thus occupied, Alison and Evie were shown around the two rooms that were for sleeping in. Then the area that Jenna called the 'lounge room', which incorporated quite a big kitchen with an electric stove, a small refrigerator containing two packets of U.H.T milk and a walk-in pantry, which still had a shelf full of food in various packaging, canisters of coffee and tea and in cupboards over the white free-standing cooker, a selection of white kitchenware, a mixing bowl and crockery.

A separate toilet, a bathroom, which had a bath, a sink and a shower cabinet, and then lo and behold, a room with a twin-tub washing machine! Though the walls could have done with a coat of paint, as there were many scuffs and dirty marks about the place, it seemed to Alison that the previous tenant had done her best to keep it nice.

The flat was fully furnished too. Not wonderfully so, as the dark brown three-seater sofa sagged in the middle, the table and upholstered chairs looked scratched and grubby and the beds were made up with sheets and blankets that had seen better days. But Evie, who was now waiting to be shown around her flat next door and always looked for the best in every situation, commented that all in all it was more than she expected and thanked a smiling Jenna for it being so.

"My sister emigrated here a few years ago and told me all sorts of tales of what the accommodation might be like when we got here, but if my flat is similar to this one, then I'll be as pleased as punch!"

Heaving a startled Joe, her elder son, out of the pedal car, much to his dismay, Evie set off with Jenna and the two boys, promising that she'd be back again later and they'd sort out some thing for their tea. Alison, on further investigation, found two drawers full of cutlery, along with a whisk and other stainless steel kitchen utensils for cooking with and half a dozen cotton tea towels and table linen. That was in addition to the cleaning cloths and liquids, she found in a washing-up bowel under the sink.

It wasn't long before Graham appeared with a self-satisfied smirk on his face.

"Silly bastards. Do yer know that the people who had this place before us, have gone back to Birmingham? The woman at the desk said they were only here for a couple of weeks and the wife missed her family. I mean, who'd want to go back to all that snow and winters that can freeze yer balls off? Don't you start fretting to go home, 'cause this is it, Alison. *We* won't be going back to Blighty with our tails between our legs. Anyway, come on, show me around the bloody place. Their loss our gain, but we'll have to get a telly. Compared to our place back home, this is like a feckin' palace!"

According to Graham, who was like a dog with two tails because of the comfortable accommodation and the enclosed communal terrace outside with a *'barbie'*, where washing could be hung and the children could play safely, they were to attend a meeting first in the morning.

"An orientation meeting, the woman said, though I'm not sure what she was going on about. I said to Tim that I couldn't understand what the Chinese had to do with anything, but Tim thinks it might be something to do with them Aborigines."

"It means finding your way around things, nothing to do with the Chinese or Aborigines."

"What does, bloody clever clogs? Oh that, anyway, after the meeting, if you want, you and his wife can have a look about. You know, find the shops first so that we can get some grub in. They've got someone to look after the kids, while we all go to the meeting and then us fellows will have our interviews. There's blokes with jobs on offer who are coming at eleven o' clock. Have you got some of those Aussie dollars I give you to hold onto? Only, the man said, there's a place down the road where we can have a drink and a bite to eat. Sandwiches and that. I told Tim that you women will bring the kids back after and put them to bed, while we have another couple of jars."

The Rose and Crown, a small hostelry a short walk away, was just what the two men were looking for. Carrying a child apiece, the two families followed the smell of a barbecue and discovered that to their delight, that this was the night when the landlord's wife did the cooking in the yard outside.

The next morning, after a good night's sleep for everyone, though Alison's body still felt a little shaky, affected as she was by the travelling from the other side of the world, the two families made their way to a local community hall. A good breakfast had been eaten by all, as the previous tenant had left behind a large box of Weetbix, two canisters of tea and coffee and two cartons of long-life milk, so these were shared with their new friends from next door.

Pandemonium was the order of the day when they arrived at the meeting. Children ran unchecked, migrants stood in groups. Although there were chairs to be had, in rows laid out in front of the stage and organisers were putting out cups of tea and plates of biscuits on a long wooden table. There were sounds of chaos, until a man of military bearing climbed upon the small stage at the back of the hall and silenced reigned. People took their seats and waited expectantly. Even the children, sensing that this was a person of authority standing before them, ran to their parents quickly.

"Good day to you all," the man began, looking around the room and speaking in a manner that made you think of a sergeant major. "Welcome to Elizabeth. I trust you all had a goodnight's sleep and are looking forward to your first day here, where you will learn something about the area, our schools, our churches and other amenities. As you may know Elizabeth was planned as a 'Garden City', built on 3,000 acres of farmland that was purchased by the South Australian Housing Trust. This was undertaken out of necessity, to house the many people who have taken up the opportunity to help build our economy. We have need of tradesmen to continue with our building programme, labourers to work in our car industry, workers are needed in our Weapons Research Establishment and there are various other subsidiary companies who need many hands. Our state government would like to say a big thank you to you all for taking advantage of our sponsorship scheme, but remember you must be prepared to work hard in your chosen field for at least two years. We do not take kindly to people who abuse our visa system for their own ends. Now, before we get started, I would like to ask our lady volunteers to lead the children to the playroom. There they will be entertained, until we have finished our orientation and have a well earned tea break."

There was a buzz of anticipation, as the children departed and the migrants waited for their next speaker to begin. Graham and Tim speculated on the type of work on offer and Alison and Evie wondered where they could find their nearest food store.

A woman whom they recognised as the person who had been standing behind the desk on their arrival, took to the stage and began to tell them about the local amenities. Freemont Park on the Main North Road had a lake and extensive gardens, which was a must for mothers and children to explore. There was an open-air shopping centre, with all the stores you would expect to be there. Including a Woolworths, which made the English women listening begin to feel at home.

There was a bank, a post office, a bakery and cafes there, and a hotel and a theatre called The Octagon nearby. Churches of most denominations were in the area and buses ran into Adelaide city centre, where more stores lay on Rundle Street. There were beautiful beaches along the coast and picnic areas, where the man of the house could barbecue.

"You Brits might have a little difficulty understanding the Aussie language at first," the woman explained, tongue in cheek as she finished off her talk. "Yes, we all speak English, not Aboriginal, but over the years words have been shortened since our civilisation of the colony began. A tradesman is called a 'tradie', a postman is a 'postie', a fireman is called a 'firie'. And if you come from Manchester, you will be puzzled when you see that our bedding is called Manchester too and that was because of the textile industry you see. Textiles were synonymous with the Manchester area, as you probably know. Now, I am sure you would like to partake of some refreshments, so have a great day and if anyone has any questions, please come and talk to me."

"I want to talk to her about where they've put us," said a young woman, who was sitting with her husband in the row of chairs behind. "We've three kids and we've been put in a two-bedroom flat. You won't be able to swing a cat in that bedroom, once Sally's out of her cot."

"Oh, Chrissie, don't make a scene, love." Her man sounded nervous. " Not today. Let's wait until I get a job and then we can look for somewhere bigger and we get to know the place better. She can stay in our room for the next few months."

"Aye, I agree with yer, mate." Graham turned around, immediately putting on his charm and speaking to the woman's husband, who was a thickset stocky man with bulging muscles. "It won't do to make a scene, not if yer want to stay put in the country. The people who had our flat before us went back after a couple of weeks. The woman said it was because the wife was missing her family, but sometimes yer don't always get to know the truth. I'm Graham Mason by the way," he held out his hand to shake their hands politely. " This is Tim, his wife Evie and Alison, my wife. Pleased to meet yer. Do yer like going out for a pint?"

It was a little while later when Alison, Evie, their children and Chrissie, who had decided to tag along with her three little girls, walked along to the shopping centre. Chrissie still complained about her flat being too small for her family, until Evie could bear it no longer and had to have her say. She suggested that Chrissie's girls slept top to toe, once little Sally grew out of her cot and joined them in their bedroom. "That's what we had to do when we were kids. There were six of us in our back-to-back terrace house in Toxteth."

Alison said nothing. She and her sister had their own spacious rooms in Redstone House, but she wasn't going to admit to that and put them off her. Even confessing to having lived on the Wirral would make her sound posh.

Chapter Fourteen

"A pipe factory, Alison. Easy as. Making fittings and pipes for use in all sorts of places. It beats driving that ruddy bus up and down past Hamilton Square each day. Tim got a job at the Holden car factory. He's working in the pressing room, but it sounded as if you need plenty of muscles to do that job and Neil, that's the bloke I was talking to this morning, is going to be out in all this hot weather, being a brickie on a tower block they've started building. Mind you, he's got to go on a training course first. Even though he was a skilled bricklayer, he's still got to learn how to do it over here. Silly feckers."

Graham got up from the sofa where he had been sitting with the children on his knees and went to get a bottle of beer from the refrigerator. He sounding elated. " I start tomorrow. It's a twelve-hour shift and I'm on early, just like I was back home. I'm to work in the tool room, but the man said if yer work hard yer can get promoted up the ladder. What to, I don't know, but the money's good. Tim won't be getting anything like the wage I'm on."

"Well as long as you don't swill the money down your neck like you did before," Alison said morosely, now suffering with a terrible headache, as she hadn't worn a sun hat when she and the others had walked in hot sunshine, along the side of the lake with the children.

Once they had done their shopping, the women had needed to keep the children occupied for the afternoon and remembered the woman talking about Freemont Park. Now all Alison wanted to do was lie down after taking a couple of aspirins, but there was tea to get and she knew that Graham didn't like waiting.

"I've found out where the rent office is, so there are no excuses."

"Bloody typical, you're never happy, Alison. I'm doing my best for you and the kids and all yer do is moan. Come on, boys, let's go and have a kick about in the yard and Ali, don't be too long making me bloody tea."

"What's this?" he asked suspiciously, when Alison presented him later with a plate of chips and a chicken schnitzel, which was a thinly sliced piece of chicken, breaded, garnished and fried. He pushed it around the plate with his knife, although the boys whose piece had been shared and cut into small portions, were eating their schnitzel enthusiastically.

"It's a schnitzel. Very popular with the Aussies, so the man at the butchers told me. You can get veal, chicken or beef I believe and the chicken variety is what Tim and Evie are having for tea, just like we are. If you want to be an Aussie, you have to eat like an Aussie. Here, have some of this sauce that the man gave me to try." Alison pushed a small tub across the table. "It's called parmegiano." She smiled to herself when Graham asked if they had a bottle of tomato sauce.

It had seemed strange that morning, she reflected later, once the children had been put to bed and Graham was sitting outside with Tim smoking their cigarettes. Shopping at the open-air mall was totally different from doing her shopping at the Co-op in Prenton. The mothers and children had wended their way along the dusty pavement, pushing the smaller children along in their fold-up prams or in Alison's case, a pushchair with Nathan aboard.

Brightly coloured parrots flew in and out of the gum trees that lined the way and white corellas squawked raucously as they winged their way overhead. The older children, who had been told about the local wildlife when they had been looked after by the volunteers, scanned the trees for koalas, who just might be sitting in the branches above. It was like as if they were on an extended holiday, according to Chrissie and the other two women agreed that it was.

Chrissie, it appeared, had also, like Evie, insisted that they seek a new life for their children. Brought up on a Salford housing estate and with Neil, her husband of eight years in and out of permanent employment as a bricklayer, Chrissie reckoned that the assisted passage offered to tradesmen like her husband should be taken advantage of.

She was a pretty girl, albeit with rather sulky features, but had a heart-shaped face, light blue eyes and blonde dyed hair that needed the roots doing. She also had an eye for the males of their group this morning, commenting on this one and that in a rather vulgar fashion, as they drank their tea together after listening to the speakers.

"You're so lucky to be married to such a handsome man like Graham," she had remarked later to Alison, just as they reached the shopping mall and the children began to run ahead into the precinct.

Alison had shaken her head in disbelief at this rather personal comment, seeing as she had only just met Chrissie a couple of hours before. *Handsome is, that handsome does*, she was about to retort in temper, but decided to rein in her frustration. It never did her any good.

No one knew Graham Mason like she did. Even his mother, who had brought up her two boys alone in virtual poverty, wouldn't have understood how he could wear a person down little by little with his insulting comments. And his thoughtlessness, his arrogance in his belief that he was better than anyone else. Yes, he was a charmer, a handsome man, but he was an empty vessel, devoid of compassion for anybody.

Though even Alison felt sorry for Graham the next day, when on his return to the flat after twelve long hours at the pipe-making factory, he looked woebegone, was covered in a white dust and feeling very sorry for himself.

"Oh God, what have I done?" he said, after he had taken a shower to remove all the irritation from his hair and body and sat at the table eating a beef stew that Alison had prepared.

"The place is full of it. Dust on the windowsills, all over the work benches, on the floors. I'm not talking dust like you get from not cleaning yer furniture, this is white stuff. You saw what it was like when I came in earlier. Even though we're given overalls, it seeps into the stuff you're wearing underneath. And there's loads of workers coughing."

"Then tell whoever's in charge that you want a move elsewhere," Alison said, unaware of the conditions that had been signed by Graham, when he was first applied to emigrate.

"Yer don't get it, do yer?" Graham jabbed his fork in her direction, raising his voice, so that even the children who were playing nearby, began to look alarmed. " Don't yer listen to anything I say, Alison? I'm stuck in the bloody job. I have to put up with it for two years because I'm on a sponsored visa, or I have to find the money to go back home."

"Sounds good to me. I never wanted to come here in the first place. I was forced into it because of the children."

"Bloody typical. Here I am, stuck in a feckin' hellhole for the next two years, while you sit around drinking tea all day with yer mates. Boot should be on the other bloody foot. You women don't know when you've got it made. Anyway, I knocked on before and Tim and Neil are coming for a bevvy with me later. I need to swill away this clagginess that I've got in me throat."

And this is how it was going to be for the foreseeable, thought Alison bleakly. Nothing will change and I may as well be back in the U.K with him, as here.

The days began to stretch interminably. Perhaps a walk to the shops where she had to get used to the Aussie dollar and work out if a loaf of bread at 21 cents was a bargain or not. A trip to the lake, a coffee morning on one another's patios, except on Chrissie's, who had a balcony upstairs. They watched as the children squabbled as they played, and listened to Chrissie moaning, as the couple's savings were fast running out and Neil was still on the training course.

Evie would run out of patience often. They were all in the same boat, they had all to sell their furniture, car if they had one and anything else that would bring in a few shillings and were all fearful that the dollars that they had exchanged in England would soon run out. Evie had mourned the loss of a beautiful china tea set, handed down through the family from a sea-faring ancestor who had brought it back from the Orient and her grandmother's bit of gold jewellery that she'd had to sell in the pawn shop.

One day, to Alison's surprise, she received a letter from her mother in the post. It was Alison's job to visit the block of mailboxes that had been provided for the occupants' use. Each flat had its own special key and number and as Graham had never been bothered about opening post, Alison had become the key holder.

They had been in the country for around four months and apart from Alison sending a postcard to her parents, with a picture of a kangaroo on the front when they had first arrived, that had been the only communication. Although she could have used the phone box on the corner and reversed the charge had she wanted to.

In those four months, things were going from bad to worse with Alison and Graham's relationship. Not that it was wonderful to begin with, but with Alison feeling fraught because Connor was having problems becoming potty-trained, leaving the urge to go until the last minute and filling up his little jocks; Nathan staggering about, now that he had learnt he had legs to walk on; and the usual arguments over the lack of money she was given to spend on food, rent and household bills. There was an extra bill now as Graham had got a television on hire purchase, so that he could watch the sport that the Aussies seemed to delight in, and because of the dust that he inhaled in his job, he was becoming an irritable stranger to her and her boys.

He and his mates had found a social club. It had been set up by the car manufacturer whom Tim now worked for and he was able to sign in a couple of visitors as well. Along with a bowling club and Elizabeth City Football Club, Graham was in his element. So whilst Alison sat in the flat each night looking after her sleeping children and watching programmes on the television that totally bored her, Graham was out enjoying himself and there was not a lot of his wages to spare.

The money he did condescend to give her was swallowed up as soon as he gave it to her. The rent on the flat, food, the bills for gas, electricity and now the television, left little for the odd packet of cigarettes she still indulged in.

That morning when Alison saw her mother's letter lying in the mailbox, along with another bill, which would have to be paid soon, was a time that would be ever imprinted in her frazzled mind. It was the beginning of her plan for freedom. Freedom at last from Graham Mason.

'Dear Alison,

I hope you have settled in to your new life in Australia and that you and the children are well. It must be nice for the boys to be able to play on the beaches and paddle in the sea. Thank you for the postcard. I should imagine that the boys will be delighted to see all the kangaroos and koala bears sitting in the trees.

Linda is going out with a nice young man called Peter Edwards. He has a very good job in Liverpool. She met him at the Equestrian Club.

Your father has decided to sell some of the land he owns so that he can take things a bit more easily. He has been complaining of chest pains recently and Dr. Barns says he is doing too much. I miss you and the children so much Alison, we never realise what we have until we've lost it.

Love from Mother.'

A wave of homesickness came over Alison as she there stood by the mailbox, smoking a cigarette with trembling fingers and reading the letter again. Pictures of Redstone House, her childhood home, came running through her mind that was full of misery. Her old bedroom with her brown one-eyed teddy bear sitting on the counterpane, where warmth from the fireplace in the winter radiated throughout the room. The large kitchen where her mother made bread and tasty dishes on an old fashioned range and the jars of jam and bottles of elderberry cordial in the pantry. The fruit picked from the blackberry or gooseberry bushes in the grounds of Beggarman's Cottage and the elderberry trees that overhung the lane. The Yorkshire pudding and onion gravy to go with the Sunday roast, which was served in the dining room that was only in use on Sundays, and a glass of parsnip wine or elderberry cordial at their evening meals, which her father brewed in his lean-to. She missed the view across the green grassy fields to the Irish Sea and the sound of the thrush and blackbirds singing in the surrounding trees. She missed the country lanes and the many nearby villages, which she had taken for granted until they had gone.

If she hadn't married Graham Mason she would still be living there as Linda did. She could be going out with someone like Peter Edwards and be a member of the Equestrian Club. She could stroll to the village and buy delicious cakes and tasty pies at Marie Duncan's bakery and peer into the window of Mrs. Thompson's wool shop, where a big old doll dressed in all her glory, sat in a large glass cabinet on display. She could have even been married to Andy instead, if she had been prepared to wait for him and perhaps gone to live in one of those posh detached houses that had been built by Harrock's Wood and her children would go to the Coombe Road school, as she had.

She looked at her watch. Mum would be cooking Dad his breakfast at this time of the day. Eight and half hours behind in the Aussie summer and ten and half hours behind in the winter and spring. He'd be sitting at the kitchen table, waiting impatiently for his plate of bacon and eggs to be placed in front of him. Probably dressed in his old blue boiler suit that he sometimes liked to wear, he would set off later in his lorry to the quarry or a building site, because she couldn't believe he would be taking things easy, even if he had sold some land.

It had briefly crossed her mind, as she walked back to the flat despondently, that he might have sold the cottage as well as the land. She hoped not, as it would have made a great, what the Aussies called, a 'doer-upper', and perhaps one day in the future, she could have been able to renovate the place herself. Because it had hit her like a flash, when Graham had spoken about the terms and conditions that he had signed for on the migrant programme, when they had first arrived in Elizabeth, that once he had signed on the dotted line, there had been nothing to stop her from staying back home.

She could have stayed in the flat, gone on the social or gone back to live with her parents and left it until the last minute before she had told him of her plans. What a fool she'd been, listening to him, listening to her mother, who had told her in no uncertain terms, that it was her duty to emigrate. She had to think of the children and go with him.

Things came to a head a few weeks later, when Evie, whose husband Tim was earning good wages at the car factory now and didn't spend most of it on beer as Graham did, asked Alison if she would like to go on the bus to the city. A break from the routine that they had all become accustomed to was a welcome distraction, and another girl, who had arrived from Stafford recently with her family and had been given a flat in the same building, was thinking of going along as well.

It was quite late one evening when Graham burst through the door, having had trouble getting his key into the lock for some reason. The children had been put to bed after watching *Skippy, the Bush Kangaroo* on the television and Alison began to worry that the pie and chips she had put in the oven to keep warm almost an hour before, wouldn't be fit for him to eat. It had happened in the past and it had put him in such a mood that he hadn't spoken to her for days. Not that she was concerned if he ignored her for any of his petty reasons, but that day she hoped to be given some of his pay.

He was looking tired, when after his shower he sat down at the table waiting for his dinner to be served. For once he hadn't gone for a drink after work, but complained that his eyes were itchy and perhaps he needed glasses and asked whether there was optician in the shopping mall.

"Bloody place, it's going to be the death of me," he said, after gulping down his food hungrily, even though Alison knew he would have had a meal at lunchtime in the canteen. "They made me stay behind and help with an order that was needed like yesterday. A bloody great load of stuff that should have been moved by a forklift truck off the pallet, not me and a couple of other blokes. I'm knackered, I couldn't lift a pint glass if I wanted to."

"Well, seeing as you're stopping in, can I have some money, Graham? Evie's asked if me and the boys would like to go on the bus to the city. It's supposed to be cooler tomorrow and she said we could have a look around a department store called David Jones that she's heard about and there might be an end of season sale. The boys'll love riding on the bus and Chrissie and the new girl are bringing their kids too. Connor hasn't been on a bus since we left home."

"Do yer think I'm made of money, Alison?" Graham got up from his chair and went to the fridge to get himself a beer. "Don't think yer going off gallivanting with yer mates to the city, yer get enough off me as it is."

"But I've promised now. Everyone's going and Connor's been jumping up and down with excitement all day." Alison felt like crying, she'd been really looking forward to the trip. A change from the daily routine that she had found herself in and maybe she could afford to treat herself to something nice if there was a sale.

"Well tough, yer not going and that'll be the end of it. Take the kids to the lake and take the football for a kick about. And don't try to get me to change my mind, 'cos I'm not listening." Frowning, he threw a twenty-dollar note onto the table. "Here, get me some packets of fags when you go to the mall tomorrow and some T-bone steak from the butchers. Tim said Evie got some for him the other week and he was well pleased with it."

How she hated his selfish ways, his dominance, his arrogant belief that because he was the breadwinner, she should do as she was told. T-bone steak indeed. On the money he gave her she could just about afford a bit of mince or some stewing steak. It wasn't as if he did without his lunch, like she did, making do with a couple of pieces of cheese on toast that she shared with Connor and Nathan. No, he'd be eating sausage and mash in the company's small canteen.

"What about the rent, Graham?" She tried to keep the anger from her voice because she knew it would only rile him. He had kept his fists to himself since they had come across to Adelaide, and she had tried hard not to provoke him. "There's only enough for the gas and lecky and a bit of shopping as well."

He threw a ten-dollar note onto the table, swearing inaudibly as he took the top off his bottle of beer. Taking a swig, he switched on the television and she knew then she had to keep her mouth shut.

She didn't struggle as he lay across her body later that night, feeling the late-night stubble on his chin lacerating her neck as he pounded into her. It was her lot in life and there wasn't much she could do about it yet, but she planned to do something about it one day.

Chapter Fifteen

On that spring day, when the sound of the cuckoo could be heard in the woods nearby, as she waited to lay her egg in an unsuspecting blackbird's nest, Alison's parents were indeed thinking about getting breakfast in the kitchen of Redstone House.

"I wonder if we'll hear from her today?" Catherine asked, sounding worried, as she bustled around the sink and the cooker, whilst Geoff opened his newspaper, which had just been posted through the front door.

"Just a postcard in all this time. It was January when they set out for the Antipodes and all we've had is a postcard. I hope she and the children have settled into their new life."

"Probably can't afford the cost of a postage stamp, knowing Graham Mason. He kept her short of money whilst she was living over here, so nothing will have changed."

"Well, I hope those boys are enjoying themselves. I looked in the atlas and they have some beautiful beaches for them to play on."

"I think you will find that where they've gone is more industrial. That's why they wanted workers, it's probably full of factories."

"But the weather will be nicer, won't it? I mean it's spring here and they've got autumn, but the boys will still be able to get out and play."

"Catherine, will you stop worrying. There's nothing you can do. If she needs us she knows where we are. We didn't force her to go to Australia."

"But I did," Catherine's voice sounded all wobbly. "I insisted that her place was with her husband, especially as she has the two boys to consider now. I didn't tell you, but when she came that day to tell us they were emigrating, I told her I thought it was a good idea to go. It would get her away from Nana Mason and she would have chance to repair her marriage with Graham."

Geoff shrugged his shoulders and began to eat the food she had set before him. *Women!*

"Oh, I'll tell him where to sling his hook in no uncertain terms, when I see him," Evie said, when she knocked on the door next day and Alison told her that Graham had said she couldn't go to the city. "The boys have been looking forward to this since yesterday and we're not going without you. Look, I'll lend you the money for the bus fares if that's the problem, but didn't he get paid yesterday?"

"Yes, but I only get enough to last me until his next wage, after I've paid the rent and the bills. I thought he might give me a bit extra to treat me and the boys when I said where we were going, but I have to get him a carton of fags and he said he wants some T-bone steak as well."

"Oh bugger that, you're coming. Chrissie's waiting and that other girl, what's she called, Mary? They're on the way to the bus stop, Chrissie said she'd meet us there."

"But I've nothing ready. I need to pack a bag with nappies for Nathan, his bottle and a juice for Connor and I've got to get our coats. It feels chilly this morning."

"Here, I'll help you." Evie was determined that her friend was going with them to the city and pushed past Alison, shoving her own boys ahead of her. "You sort the kid's stuff out and I'll get their coats and do you want that black jacket you've started wearing?"

"He'll go mad, if he knows that I've gone with you, Evie and if I'm not back by teatime he'll probably clock me one."

"Don't be daft, he wouldn't dare. Honest, Alison, you want to stand up to him, you're not doing much for women's liberation. Anyway, we'll be home by three or four and he doesn't get home until six at the earliest and you can get his fags in the city and it'll probably be cheaper to get him the steak from the market. Hey, why don't we get one of those new lottery tickets whilst we're there and then you could leave the bastard behind to rot."

"It's alright for you, Evie," Alison said, as they walked along to the bus stop. "Your Tim is a really nice fellow. He wouldn't start insulting you in front of everybody like Graham does. I was really upset the other night, when we were round at yours. I only said that I wondered if the returning soldiers from Vietnam would be given any of the labouring jobs in Elizabeth. I mean that sewing machine company's gone and closed recently, so those workers will be looking for something too. I was only trying to contribute to the conversation."

"You're too soft that's your problem, Alison. Stick up for yourself like I do. I tell you, your Graham would have a black eye if he spoke to me like he does to you. Anyway, cheer up, the bus will be here in a minute and we'll go off and have a good day."

The city was a beautiful place, thought Alison, when the bus dropped them at the beginning of King William Street. Elegant stone buildings lined the wide thoroughfares, some three or four storeys high with a wide veranda, and some of them had shops selling all kinds of products underneath. They intended to head for Rundle Street, though it had been decided that because they had eight children between them, some of them already cranky after their initial excitement of riding on a bus, they would split up and meet on the banks of the Torrens River later, whereever that might be.

The pavements were crowded as they trailed along the pavements, holding their children firmly by the hand, or in Evie's case holding onto the reins that she had strapped around her boys. They looked with interest at the occasional cob and stone buildings, which had probably been there since a pioneer called

Colonel Light had settled in Adelaide. Office workers scurried in dark pin-striped suits, whilst women wearing smart skirts and matching jackets, accessorised hats and gloves, tottered by on high-heeled shoes to do their shopping. Alison felt like a pauper as she compared her shabby denim skirt, her scuffed flatties and her white short-sleeved blouse, to all these well-dressed people.

They waited at a junction where a policeman on point duty controlled the heavy traffic and stared with delight at the trolley buses that were rattling by on the tramlines, full of passengers. It was a different world, the opposite of the scruffy streets of Birkenhead or Liverpool, even the shops looked classier as they wandered into Rundle Street.

And that had been the problem, thought Alison later, as they all met up on the riverbank and the children ran about on the green open spaces, wanting to know why they couldn't have a ride in one of the rowing boats that were moored nearby. Classy shops meant spending money that she didn't have and probably never would whilst she was married to Graham Mason. A cheese sandwich and a glass of lemonade, bought in Coles' cafeteria and shared between Connor and Nathan, had cost an arm and a leg and the bargain rail in the department store held nothing on offer that she could afford.

It was hard for her to see that both Chrissie and Mary were carrying brown paper carrier bags and their children carried brown floppy-eared kangaroos or cuddly koala toys that their mothers had bought them, whilst she held onto her tatty old handbag with just her housekeeping in and her boys had nothing at all.

'Harris Scarfe' Mary, a thin young woman with a five-year-old daughter said, pulling out a pretty patterned dress and showing it to the others proudly, "Two dollars and I got her a pair of school shoes too. She'll be going to school in October. You know, that one that's just opened on Canberra Road." The others nodded. All their children would be going to Canberra Road, none of them could afford to educate them privately.

"And I got a scarf from Harris Scarfe," Chrissie quipped,

pulling out a thin gauzy piece of material and showing it to them proudly. "Anyway, where next? Don't forget we've only another hour or so to do our shopping."

"I thought the market on Grote Street next," Chrissie ventured. "I've heard they sell homegrown stuff from local allotments and there's a couple of butchers and stalls selling different types of cheese. Neil loves Camembert. Someone said there's a Chinese archway just in front of the entrance. We could have a look at that too."

"Sounds good to me," said Evie, knowing that Alison had little money and it must be difficult for her having to do only window shopping. She had refrained from buying a pair of summer sandals in the David Jones sale because of it, nor a toy apiece for the children, although Tim had given her a five-dollar note to treat herself and her boys.

"Come on then, let's get going," Chrissie shouted, as the two eldest boys and one of Chrissie's girls came rolling down the hill, much to their mothers' annoyance. Grass stains on their bodies and clothes were all they needed and if it hadn't been for Mary's quick-thinking action, one of the children might have fallen into the river, he was giggling so helplessly.

"We might be able to get a cup of tea," Chrissie said, as they struggled along near Victoria Square, the children who were walking, trudging now as the trip to the city had been very tiring. "There's sure to be a cafe and we can get the kids a drink."

Sods Law! It had to be the day when the management at the pipe factory had decided that the labourers in the tool room could leave early, because they had stayed late the day before. Graham was standing outside the door of their flat, looking unwashed, unshaven and his denim work clothes and steel-capped boots were covered in the usual layer of white dust. He scowled at Alison as he took away the cigarette from his lips, but smiled when Connor raced to greet him.

"Where've you been?" he asked, as his eldest hugged his leg

lovingly. "We've been on a bus, Daddy and it went a long, long way to the city. Then we had to walk miles and miles. Then we played by a river, then we saw a great big lion with red lanterns. That's what Mummy called them, red lanterns."

"Oh she did, did she?"

Chrissie and Mary waved goodbye and hurried off with their children and their carrier bags full of food, that they had bought at the Central Market. It didn't do to get involved in a domestic and it looked as if someone was going to get it in the neck.

"You can blame me," Evie said gaily, as Alison wheeled the pushchair towards him with little Nathan inside and Evie's boys still with their harnesses on at her side. "We all needed a break and I persuaded Ali to come with us. We've had a lovely day. Maybe when the weather gets warmer, we can all go to the beach."

"Aye maybe," Graham said, lifting Nathan out of his pushchair and giving him a cuddle. "Anyway, tell Tim that I'll be over at the Rose and Crown this evening. It'll mek a change from the Club."

"I got your fags and your T-bone steak, Graham," Alison said, as the family walked into the flat and she put her purchases onto the kitchen counter. "I couldn't get you any Embassy Regal, so as there was a promotion on these Pall Mall cigarettes, I bought you them instead."

She busied herself. From the look on his face, he was working himself up into a temper. Lighting the gas with a match, she turned to put the kettle she had just filled up with water on top of the stove.

"Since when have I ever smoked anything other than Embassy Regal, Alison?" He put little Nathan down and told the boys to play outside.

"You used to smoke Embassy Red. Ouch! Graham, you nearly made me burn myself on the gas flame. Oww! For God's sake stop hurting me, I thought you'd like these with them being American."

"I ought to wring your bloody neck, you little bitch," he hissed at her. "I told yer last night you weren't to go to the city and what do I find when I get home early, yer go behind me back. If it wasn't for the kids, I'd give yer a bloody slap that yer wouldn't forget in a hurry. Now I'm going for a shower and I want my dinner waiting on the table when I'm finished and yer can open a bottle of beer to go with it. And none of that feckin' rabbit food, I want chips."

The tears of frustration came later, as she bathed the boys together and played splashing games. She rubbed her arm, as she kneeled beside them, knowing that there would be a purple bruise by the morning and she would have to wear her only long-sleeved jumper to cover it. Graham had got worse since starting at the pipe factory and from the state he came in from the ale house sometimes, he was beginning to drink too much. How could he begrudge her one nice day out, when she hadn't spent a cent on herself or the children?

She couldn't go on. One day he would end up killing her, then the boys would be without a father as he rotted in jail and then where would the poor kids be?

'Dear Mum and Dad,
Thank you for your letter. I'm sorry that I've been so long in replying, but…'

But what? Alison chewed on her pen, waiting for words to flow, so that she could tell her parents why she hadn't written. She hadn't any writing paper or an envelope or money to buy a stamp?

'… but the days are so busy, I keep meeting myself coming back! We have a nice flat near a park, which the boys love to race around in. Nathan is growing fast and I've finally got Connor out of nappies. I've made some good friends. Evie is my best friend and the other two girls are Chrissie and Mary. Evie's husband works in a car factory, as does Mary's husband but in a different section. Chrissie's husband is working on a high-rise block of flats, that will probably be so high up, you can see over to the ocean. Graham is working in a factory where they make pipe fittings and pipes. He

145

doesn't like it and he comes home covered in a white dust. He has to work for two years there before he can look for something else. Each day I pray that he'll want to move back to England.

I miss you Mum and Dad,

Love from Alison.

P.S Tell Linda I miss her too.'

It was the middle of July when Catherine sat down to read the letter from her daughter. It was six and a half months since Alison and the boys had gone away and she found she was really missing them. In that time, Linda had become engaged to Peter Edwards and a slap-up wedding was in the planning stage and scheduled for the following June. The ceremony was to take place at St. Bartholomew in Thurstaston and the reception was to be held at the Parkgate Hotel. Peter's parents who lived in Gayton were from a rather well-to-do family, who had made their money in shipping.

From the tone of Alison's letter it appeared that the girl had settled to her new life out there in Adelaide, but there seemed to be a fly in the ointment with Graham not liking his job. Perhaps in two years time, God willing, they would return to live in England. Perhaps they could be helped to get a mortgage, now that Geoffrey had a lot of money from the land he had sold, which was only lying in the bank.

In Catherine's reply, she mentioned that a wedding invitation would be coming in the post to Alison. Although she knew that the couple wouldn't be able to attend the ceremony, which was a shame as she missed her little grandchildren.

Chapter Sixteen

It was cold that July in the Adelaide winter. The flat was always chilly even though Graham had purchased a paraffin heater to warm up the place and most days were around forty-five degrees. She knew that he had only bought it, because he was staying up late watching England play cricket against the West Indies at Lords and that was when the flat was at its coldest at night.

Alison had found a shop that sold once worn clothing for a very small price, so she was able to buy winter jackets for the boys and herself. Although it rained sometimes, it kept the grass in the parkland and the gum trees that lined the roads well watered, but it made it hard to dry the clothes when she did her daily wash.

It had been a couple of days since she had received Linda and Peter's wedding invitation and a germ of an idea in her mind had been festering. She hugged herself in her fleece-lined duffle coat which she had begun to wear indoors, as well as a thick jumper and denim jeans, and dared herself to believe that she could carry out her plans.

She didn't bother to show her husband the pretty card, which somebody, perhaps Linda who had a flair for artistry, had probably spent hours designing. What was the point? Graham would only say what she knew already, that they hadn't got the money to throw away on fares and who would want to travel back to England for a snotty wedding anyway?

Well, *she* would and with all the money that her father must have made from the sale of some land and probably Beggarman's

Cottage, she could very likely persuade him to send some of it her way. Especially as he hadn't paid a penny towards her own wedding and as Linda's would probably be a society do, his conscience just might prick him. It was her chance to leave Graham Mason forever. Take the boys with her and return to the home that she loved.

The months crawled by and Alison, impatient to put her plan into operation had written to her mother accepting the invitation to Linda and Peter's wedding and asked if it was possible for her father to help with the fares. She felt excited, but worried in equal measures, but surely her plans to leave her husband would be foolproof. Dad was bound to send her some money, but would she and the children be allowed to leave the country? Were she and the children signed up to the migrant programme too?

"I don't think so," said Evie thoughtfully, when Alison invited her neighbour around for a coffee one morning in early December to pick her brains and for the boys to have a little playtime together as well. "I think it's Graham who wouldn't be allowed to leave the country, if he wanted to keep his two-year sponsorship. If he did leave, he'd probably have to repay an awful lot of money back to the government. Why, are you thinking of scuttling back to Blighty? I'd hate to go back, especially with the summer coming up in Adelaide."

"Well, I suppose I'm going to have to tell you sometime, Evie. Seeing as you're my best friend, that is. My sister Linda is getting married next June and I'm sure my Dad will pay for our flights there, but I know he wouldn't want Graham to come back for the wedding as well."

"Didn't they get on?"

"They hated each other. Dad thought I had one leg in the gutter by marrying a bus driver, especially as I went to grammar school. And Graham in return, hated Dad because he knew in his eyes, he wasn't good enough."

"Oh dear. Not a good basis for a happy marriage, if you don't mind me saying so. No wonder Graham treats you like he does.

Deep down he probably thinks that you feel the same way about him, as your Dad does."

"Since when did you become a philosopher?" Alison laughed, offering her friend a plate of Oreo cream-filled biscuits, that she had bought the day before, and taking one to eat herself. "Mmm, chocolate, no wonder I can't lose weight with having to eat these kind of biscuits. But the kids love them."

"Yes, you have put on a bit of weight, haven't you, Alison? I was only thinking that the other day, when you were complaining your jeans were getting tight around the backside."

"No, they shrunk in the wash – I've never really got used to the temperature settings. Anyway, will you keep our tête-a-tête a secret for the moment? I have to see how much the flights cost first, as they might be astronomical for Connor, Nathan and me. If Graham hears what I'm planning to do too early, he won't let me go."

"He probably won't anyway. Remember that stink when we went up to the city that day?"

"He's never let me forget it, Evie."

"Anyway, I've got some news if you're interested. Tim's being allowed to buy a car through Holden. He hasn't decided what he wants yet, but with me being able to drive as well, I'm going to get a say!"

"Wow! Gosh, you're so lucky. I suppose Graham'll be wanting one next, though he doesn't need one, working so close."

"Just in time for Christmas," Evie said gleefully. "Though it's going to be strange having Christmas here instead of England. I always think of Santa Claus and snow. Have you got your cards ready to send back to England? Only I've heard it is rather snail mail."

"Yes," Alison said sadly. "I've sent them, but they weren't very Christmassy. I bought a pack and they were all pictures of assorted beaches. Luckily I didn't have so many people to send them to. Just family, parents, sister, relatives who lived up the road from me and Gaynor my best friend."

"Not one to Graham's family then?" Evie had been told all about how she was chucked out of the flat by Nana Mason. Alison shook her head.

"It's up to him, I won't send her one. It cost me enough for cards and stamps for my lot as it is. Then there's all the food to buy for Christmas Day and presents for the kids. I don't know how I'm going to be able to afford it this year."

"And we won't be here to celebrate," Evie said, although she didn't sound regretful. "We're off to Whyalla. With Tim getting the car, we can go to our Brenda's and stay for a couple of days. It'll be great seeing her and the kids again. Anyway, perhaps you and Chrissie could organise a get-together for everyone here on Christmas Day. You know, use that barbecue out there on the terrace for the men to do some cooking and all *you* have to do is take along a contribution. BYO, I think the Aussies call it."

It was around about that time, that Graham developed a cough, which kept them awake at night and made him cranky. It was also around that time that Alison had the suspicion that she may be pregnant, especially after Evie had remarked about her weight and a couple of mornings recently, she'd been feeling queasy. How many weeks she didn't know, as her periods had always been erratic and Graham had never worn protection.

It hadn't helped his mood when Alison suggested that perhaps they could make a New Year resolution and give their lungs a bit of a breather the following year. They had both been smokers from an early age and she had begun to think of the health of her and her baby and the money they would save.

"Perhaps we could have a day out by the sea, or a couple of days on the Eire Peninsula, where Evie and Tim are going for Christmas with what we save," Alison had said glibly. "We haven't been anywhere as a family and Evie says there are a lot of nice beaches only an hour away from here."

"Aye, well it's alright for them who can afford it, Alison. I mean Tim's being given the chance of getting a car at a cheaper price, hasn't he? A perk of the job, not something the company I work for would ever consider." He lit a cigarette and she noticed that his hand was shaking slightly. "Anyway, if I wanted to pack it up, I can, easy. Let's face it, if I didn't have me fags and the odd bottle of beer now and again, what's the point of getting out of bed?"

"The migrant programme, that's a good enough reason. You've still another year to do."

She knew then why his hand was shaking as he had lit his cigarette. He'd been trying to keep his temper in, as the children were eating their bowls of cereal nearby and were watching the television. To give Graham his due, he tried not to be angry in front of the children.

"Don't lecture me, Alison," he said menacingly, pushing her across towards the kitchen counter, out of earshot of the boys. "Don't I bloody know that I signed up to the wrong job, instead of going after one at Holden. At the time I thought a ten-hour shift making a few pipes for the building trade would be easy. The pay's good, but I hate it there. It's worse than driving a bus around and around the Oxton Circle. At least I had lots of time at the terminus if I put my foot down."

"We could always go back to England. I'm sure they'd give you some training on those new buses if you wanted, or you could always go and work at Vauxhall making cars." *And I can have my baby there, and it won't be born on Australian soil.*

"Oh feck off, will yer. If yer think I'm going to trail back home and have me mates saying I couldn't hack it, you've got another thing coming. Besides, I've no money to pay the government back nor our airfares."

"Dad might help us."

"As I said before, feck off, Alison."

It was a few days later when a brown envelope addressed to Alison came into her mailbox. There was a letter inside a Christmas card, which showed a robin redbreast sitting on a Royal Mail post box, covered in snow, outside a thatched cottage. Attached to the letter was a bank draft for $2,500. Alison's heart did a somersault.

Dear Alison,

We trust that you and the boys are well and you will by now have found the bank draft that your father has organised for you. Of course we will be very happy to see you and the boys again, but it is a pity that Graham cannot travel with you. I am sure his mother and brother would have been pleased to see him again. However, I am sure you are capable of travelling with the boys on your own and there will be airline staff who will help if you ask them. That is what they are paid to do.

You didn't say when we can expect you, Alison. Will you be coming for a little holiday before the wedding and perhaps stay after for a couple of weeks as well? It seems such a waste of all that money if you and the boys were only to stay just for the ceremony. There is ample room at Redstone House, now that Linda and Peter have purchased one of those nice properties on Thorstone Drive.

Things are in hand for their wedding. Linda wondered if you would like to be her maid of honour. If you agree, you will be wearing blue. That is her colour scheme for the whole celebration. Even the men, including Peter, are having matching waistcoats and ties with their morning suits.

Your father said that you should let him know if the enclosed draft isn't enough for the airfares, although a little extra has been added for you to buy Christmas presents from us for the boys. He went to Thomas Cook's in Liverpool and they thought that it should be plenty. If not you can make a reverse trunk call to our telephone number. You are to present the draft at your local bank and they will do the necessary.

It won't be long before we see you again. We are all looking forward to it.

Love and kisses to the boys and a Happy Christmas.
Mother.

Alison's heart was thumping as she and the children entered the Bendigo Bank next morning. She clutched her tattered handbag, which held the bank draft, her birth certificate and her passport, closer to her chest. She had prepared for every possibility, as nothing, even Graham Mason was going to stand in her way and had hidden the bank draft overnight in her vanity bag, which had been a present from her mother as a going-away gift.

Graham hadn't even bothered to comment, when she had told him that she thought she might be expecting. She had felt him shrug his shoulders and then, unusually for him, as he still expected sex most evenings, had turned away from her in bed. Not that she minded, as she hated his unwanted fumbling, especially when he had been drinking and had beer-smelling breath. But what she did mind was having to go through an unwelcome pregnancy.

According to the conversations that her friends from the flats sometimes indulged in, there were ways and means of not falling for a baby each year and Alison listened avidly, since she hadn't got the money to pay for birth pills. Mary, whose husband worked as a brickie and was so tired when he came home that he seldom indulged her, said that when he did, he used a johnny, but it had taken her ages anyway to conceive her daughter, Julia

Chrissie, who had three young children had said that she wasn't bothered about contraception, the more the merrier in her family, but if she did, she'd see the doctor about getting the contraceptive pill. Evie recommended the douche, although it was a nuisance having to get out of the bed in the middle of the night to use it. Alison and Graham never used a thing after he had thrown away her pills that time. He thought it was an insult to his manhood.

It had been a strange kind of Christmas, Alison mused, as she picked up the money from the bank draft, once the festive season was over and normal hours of working were resumed. Strange in that it was celebrated on a day when the sun was cracking the flags and everyone invited from the building on Christmas Day had appeared in summer shorts and tops. With the obligatory hat and sunglasses resting on their heads, of course.

It was strange to eat a hot dog covered in tangy yellow mustard;

a seared piece of chicken, that was dry and overcooked; T-bone steaks that were cremated; or lightly burnt corn on the cob. She had longed for a roast turkey dinner with cranberry sauce and all the trimmings and a plum pudding with a brandy custard, not a raspberry cheesecake or a piece of strawberry pavlova and thick double cream.

The children had worn reindeer ears, instead of paper hats from a box of crackers and she hadn't sung any carols, which she would have done at home. There were platters of crispy-looking potato skins, dishes of dips and coleslaw, bowls of salad and plates of cheese. The men drank beer whilst they took their turn at the barbecue and the children ate copious amounts of chocolate orange, Ritz crackers, crisps and fizzy pop.

Her present from Graham had nearly been her undoing. Along with a go-cart for the boys and a Meccano set, he had given her a coat. It was a light blue woollen coat with four large self-coloured buttons and an ornamental rose as a fastener at the throat. She had felt overwhelmed, especially because she had only bought him a bottle of Hi Karate and had felt like crying, because of her guilt. Then he told her he had got her coat and the boy's gifts from a mail order catalogue and she could now take over the payments, that he had been making every week.

It had made her blood boil and reinforced her conviction that she couldn't live the rest of her life with Graham Mason. She was sure she would be in an early grave if she stayed with him.

Chapter Seventeen

It was in the January of 1970, the year that the Apollo 13 splashed down safely in the Pacific and Dana won the Eurovision Contest on behalf of Ireland, that Alison finally decided to purchase her tickets back home for herself and the boys. Well, not for Nathan, he was under two and would sit in a bassinet or on her knee for most of the journey. The bank draft, which had been waiting to be cleared, had now been turned into lots of different kinds of dollar notes and been handed over to the woman in the travel agents. The flight was booked for Wednesday 1st April; perhaps a fool's day for some, but not for Alison.

Her husband was a tosser, or a bogan as people in Australia would have called him, if they had known what he was like. He had five-star tastes on a two-star income and Alison was heartily sick of it.

His latest want had been a new car like the one Tim had bought at factory prices. Tim's was a Holden Belmont, a four-door sedan in a light brown colour. It was parked outside in front of the building and Graham cast envious eyes in its direction every time he passed it by. When Alison had reminded him gently that his place of work was only a ten-minute walk away and the purchase of a car on their limited income would be suicidal, he'd gone mental. And if she had any doubts before about leaving him to his own devices, they had flown into the ether after his latest trick.

That evening as he had walked through the door, as usual

covered in a white dust and desperate for a beer to clear his throat, he had told her that he was going that weekend to a car showroom, with one of his mates.

"I've decided that if I can get one on the never never, I'm going for it. I work bloody hard at that sodding factory and a man has to have some compensations in life."

Alison was livid.

"And where's the money coming from to pay for it, Graham?" she asked, trying to keep her voice low, as the children were watching *Andy Pandy* on the television. "We're already up to our necks in debt since you bought the TV and I'm still paying off that catalogue money for the Christmas presents. Anyway, you'll have to pack up smoking and cut back on the beer if you want a car. If I've had to pack up smoking with being pregnant, so can you."

"Who earns the bloody money, Alison? What have you ever contributed to this marriage since we got wed?"

"Err, two kids and one on the way Graham and don't forget you didn't want me working in the first place."

"Well, you'll have to now. They want cleaners at the factory a couple of days a week. You can go and see the foreman next Monday. I'll know how much the repayments will be by then and if it's more than I think, you can ask for extra hours."

"And who'll be looking after Connor and Nathan, while I'm out keeping you in the lap of luxury?" she asked sarcastically.

"You can ask one of your mates. They've nothing else to do except to look after their own kids. You can bung them a few dollars a week. Anyway, one of the lads from work is looking to buy a car as well, so we'll make a day of it. We might go up to the city and look at some of the car dealers there."

Alison shook her head disbelievingly, feeling cheesed off with it all.

It was just before Easter when Graham began to have his coughing fits. Bad ones when he sounded as if he was going to choke. Alison had managed to sidestep his wish for her to clean at the factory, citing her need to be there for her boys, instead of farming them out with her friends. Connor had become rather clingy recently and she wondered if he could feel her anticipation that was building up inside. In a few days time she would be winging her way to freedom, hopefully never to set her eyes again on Graham Mason.

Her few possessions were packed and hidden in her suitcase at the back of the fitted wardrobe in the boys' room. Her vanity bag was full of toiletries, a pack of disposable nappies, a jar of zinc and caster oil ointment, plenty of tissues and baby wipes. It only remained for her to pick up the tickets from the travel agent, which she was to do on Tuesday morning. Her fervent hope was that Graham didn't decide to go on the sick. If he did, then she was scuppered.

He had got his wish. A brand new Ford Falcon XR 500 station wagon with a white roof and a brown body, was now parked behind Tim's Holden and once filled up with 'gas' from the 'bowser' Graham became a happy man. He had even driven them to the coastal town of Glenelg one evening, where settlers, not convicts had colonised the area in 1839.

It was on that day, if she'd had any doubts about leaving him, that Alison finally decided that there was no point in her and Graham's relationship anymore. As they sat side by side in silence on the sands, whilst other families played ball games, happily chivvying each other on, Graham sipped from a bottle of beer and smoked a cigarette, whilst looking out across the Gulf of St.Vincent towards the Yorke Peninsular. Alison, keeping an eye on the boys, who were digging a hole with a couple of spoons she had brought along with her, as she had no money to buy them buckets and spades, knew then that she was making the right decision to go home.

She didn't really know him. They had nothing in common other than the children and it felt like she was living with a stranger most of the time. A handsome man who had drawn her into his web of superficial charm and she had fallen for it. Their life together based on sex and children and nothing more. He wouldn't grieve when he realised that she had left him. He would pick himself up, get on with his life and would probably find some other poor woman to dominate in time.

Evie, who hadn't been told the real truth, in case she unwittingly spilled the beans to her husband, and had only been told that Alison's father had paid for their flights to go to her sister's wedding and they would be back soon, was there to say goodbye on the morning of their departure. Along with Chrissie, Mary, their children and another few women from their building, Alison and the boys were waved off in a taxi that would take them to the airport for their flight.

It had been touch and go when Graham began another coughing fit the night before their departure, leaving Alison pacing the kitchen floor in a panic and unable to sleep. What if he decided to spend the day in bed, instead of working? What if he decided to visit the doctor and was given a sick note?

She wondered again, her conscience pricking for the hundredth time, if it was wrong of her to take his little boys and start another life without him. But this was his punishment, his come- upperance in Alison's eyes. This was pay back time for the way that she had been treated, since he married her.

Connor, all excited, as he climbed aboard the taxi along with Nathan who was now toddling, clutched a little rucksack with a furry koala on the front, which had been bought for Christmas with some of her father's money. Inside there was a change of underwear, a small bottle of pop and a bottle of milk for Nathan, a couple of bibs and his favourite teddy. She had told him only that morning that they were going away on holiday and with Graham not due home until the evening, they'd soon be far away.

It was a tired, but happy Alison when the plane touched down in Gatwick a couple of days later. A long wait in the international airport at Sydney had frayed her nerves, made her boys fractious and Connor, who had appeared to be affected by the change in air pressure in the cabin of the 747, was also glad to be on *terra firma* again.

The cabin crew, used to wailing children who couldn't understand why their ears were suddenly hurting and were strapped in their seats in cramped conditions for most of the journey, were kind and understanding. Connor was put in charge of handing out the packets of peanuts or biscuits to the passengers and it took his mind off his problems, at least for a while.

In the letter that Alison had posted to her parents a couple of weeks earlier, advising them of the flight times on the date of her journey, she had written that they would make their way by train to Liverpool and could they telephone Lime Street station to check on the time of the London train. By changing her dollars to sterling at the currency exchange office in the arrivals lounge, she would have enough money for tickets for their ongoing trip.

It seemed surreal somehow, a dream that she would suddenly wake from. Her parents waiting at the barrier, as the train came to a halt at the side of the platform, its steam whooshing and the engine clanking, causing Nathan to cling to Alison in fright. Her parents were looking anxious, as they searched the surging crowd for their daughter and two little grandsons and it came to her in a tumble of emotions, what she must have put them through: her choice of men, who they had never approved of, her poor choice of son-in-law, their heartbreak, especially her mother's, when she had been told by her eldest daughter that she would never see her grandchildren again.

For that is what Alison had said before they parted. Angry, because her mother had insisted that her place was with her husband and that it seemed a good idea to emigrate and give their marriage a better chance, without having interfering Nana Mason in their life, Alison had hit back at her mother. Wanting to hurt her loved one, because she was getting the feeling that no one in her family had ever cared much about her anyway. Had it always been like that, she wondered? Had she always felt that all their love had been given to Linda, her younger sister? Perhaps it was so.

But when had they got older? When had her mother's hair turned grey and her father, his light brown hair receding and, usually slender, developed a paunch? She dashed back her tears, as her father enfolded her in his arms and her mother caught hold of the hands of Connor and Nathan, after she had hugged them.

"So you're back then?" her father said, with a tiny inflection of humour in his voice, as he held her at arm's length and gazed upon her. "Come to lead me a rare old dance and turn my hair to silver."

She shook her head wryly and her mother hugged her briefly, raising a quizzical eye as she felt her daughter's thickened waist against her own. And that was the day when Alison felt her baby quicken in her womb.

Father had changed his Morris Traveller for a smart beige Morris Marina. Big enough to hold both the family in it and a couple of suitcases in the boot, it had been a pleasant experience to travel through the Mersey tunnel again. It was growing dark, as it was only early April, but Alison could see the outlines of the many terraced houses that lined both Borough Road and Singleton Avenue and the Technical College, where she hoped to study for her O levels one day.

This was home; this was where she wanted to be with her children. Not across the world in a place that was alien and nothing was familiar, except Graham Mason. She wondered what her parents would say, when she told them that she had left him for good.

Catherine kept up a stream of nervous conversation, as she sat with little Nathan on her knee in the rear of the car, with Connor snuggled up beside her. She had spent all day getting the boys' room ready, with a bed for Connor and the old cot that first Alison and then Linda used to sleep in, for Nathan. They had been out and bought a safety gate from the new shop called

Mothercare, as Catherine knew that both her grandsons had only known accommodation without stairs and she had worried that they might fall down them. Alison was to have her old room and Geoffrey had spent the week before giving the walls a coat of paint. They hoped she still liked yellow, as it matched the new curtains and the counterpane they had bought for her.

Then her father had mentioned that a new Mersey tunnel called the Kingsway was to be opened by the Queen in June the following year and it would then be much quicker to come home via Wallasey, as they could drive along the motorway to Arrow Park. Alison remembered. They had been building the road that was to be named the M53, alongside the council estate, where she and Graham had lived with Connor in the high-rise block of flats.

Linda's fiancé, Peter, who was also a leader of a group of boy scouts, had expressed an interest in walking through the tunnel, as the public were being permitted to do before its official opening. Her parents' voices were soothing and oh, so familiar and she knew then in her heart that her home in Mill Hill was where she and her boys should be.

It was good to be eating supper back in the kitchen of Redstone House. A plate of warming scouse and slices of bread and butter was enjoyed by them all, although the boys didn't like eating the beetroot which accompanied it. They looked shattered and it wasn't too long before they were tucked up cosily in their little bedroom, although Connor kept asking where his daddy was and when they would see him? Alison kept repeating the same sentence since they got in the Adelaide taxi, that they were having a little holiday.

"Well, Connor's kept his fair hair, Alison," her mother said, as they all sat in front of the log fire later in the sitting room, drinking a glass each of Geoffrey's elderberry cordial that had just been pronounced palatable. "I thought he'd go darker like you did and Nathan takes after Grandad, with his light brown hair. Not a bit of Graham Mason in him, thank goodness. Anyway, I couldn't help noticing that you have put on a considerable amount of weight, Alison. Is there something you would like to tell us?"

Alison laughed. "You couldn't help but notice, Mother. I thought you'd guessed when you met us at the station. Yes, I think I'm about five months. I won't be able to get into the maid of honour dress if Linda got one for me."

"Well, luckily she didn't, Alison. She was waiting until you got here and then she was going to take you to the dressmakers. So, we're going to be grandparents again, Geoffrey, thanks to our prolific daughter."

Geoffrey grunted, as he poured himself another drink from one of the bottles on the wooden trolley near the stone surround fireplace.

"If prolific means what I think it means, I'd get that Graham Mason seen to, if I were you."

"I've left him, Dad." Alison thought she might as well get it over and done with. Her parents would have to know fairly soon. "So it doesn't matter to me whether he gets the snip or not, as I'm not going back to Australia."

Catherine looked horrified. "Does he know? Does he know you won't be going back after Linda's wedding? Well, you couldn't in your condition anyway, they wouldn't let you on the plane. Oh, don't tell me it's due in June."

"What's due in June?" Linda walked through the door, after taking her coat off and hanging it in the cloakroom.

"Ah the rover has returned," she said rather sarcastically, when she saw her sister. "What time did you get here?" Alison got up from the armchair to give her a hug, noticing that her blonde-haired sister had a sparkle about her. Being engaged to Peter Edwards must be doing her good.

"Not another one," she remarked, holding onto Alison's shoulders, standing back and looking at her critically. "Is that what I heard Mother saying, you're having it in June?"

"Well, I haven't seen a doctor yet, it could be May or even July. I thought I'd make an appointment with Doctor Barns, when I got here. I was frightened of getting involved in the system over there."

"It's Doctor Roberts now," Geoffrey said inconsequentially. "Nice man, saw him just the other day going up Billy Thompson's path. Do you know, Billy's nearly ninety?"

"Anyway, you won't be able to be my maid of honour looking like that, Alison. Good job I didn't get you a dress." Linda sounded relieved. She was quite happy with the three girlfriends she had chosen.

"Perhaps Connor could be a pageboy instead," Catherine said happily. "He would look really cute in a little outfit. I saw them when I was in the Co-op department store the other day."

"No, I'm happy with things as they are, Mother. Alison, would you like to take a look at my engagement ring?"

And the large diamond in a cluster was beautiful, thought Alison later, as she lay in her bed feeling a sense of contentment, though worn out with all the travelling. Compared to the garnet she wore on her finger that Graham had given her, Peter must be worth a bob or two.

Chapter Eighteen

It was good to lie in her bed that next morning listening to the boys as, fully recovered from their journey, they ran up and down the hall landing, waiting for someone to open the safety gate. She could smell bacon cooking downstairs in the kitchen and Linda or someone running a bath. Alison stretched luxuriously, then noticed that her mother had laid out one of her old dressing gowns across the back of the wicker chair, so she got out of bed and put it on gratefully.

"Mummeee!" Connor and Nathan burst into her bedroom, the door having obviously been opened by the irritated occupier of the bathroom. Nathan, with his wet nappy trailing and Connor's hair standing on his head like a bantam cock, leapt and bounced about like two excited puppies. They had both missed their mummy, as back at the flat they were allowed to run into her bedroom and snuggle down next to her in bed. House rules had to be followed though in Redstone House, as all of those who lived there, kept their bedroom doors closed at night.

It was half an hour later before the newly arrived occupants appeared washed and dressed and hungry for their breakfast. Linda, taking her time, as she wasn't due to continue her course at Carlett Park until the following Monday, where she was studying business and economics and was meeting her fiancé in Chester at lunchtime, took ages doing her ablutions in the bathroom. Luckily for the newcomers there was the downstairs cloakroom, with a washbasin and a loo.

"I see Tommy Parkinson is going to grow runner beans in his market garden this year," Geoffrey remarked, when Catherine had removed his greasy breakfast plate, then put a couple of bowls of cornflakes and milk in front of Connor and Nathan. "I saw him setting up a row of wigwams. It'll be them or broad beans. Last autumn he put in wintering cauli's and cabbages and he must have made a bomb selling all that fruit from the orchard."

"Oh yes, where's that then?" asked Alison, as she munched on a plate of scrambled eggs on toast. Tommy Parkinson. She was sure she had gone to school with his son. She supposed there would be a lot of catching up to do with all the local gossip.

"Next door. That's who I sold the land to. Didn't your mother tell you in her letter?"

"Yes," Alison replied slowly. "She said that you'd sold some land. Has he taken over the cottage as well, because I quite fancied doing it up and moving in there myself one day." She looked from face to face of her parents, who had the grace to look uncomfortable. "What?"

"It's gone," said Catherine, turning away, so Alison couldn't see her embarrassment. She had always felt guilty that it was because of what she had said the cottage was there no longer.

"Yes, it was falling to pieces and there could have been an accident with the chimney sloping like it had." Geoffrey blustered as he said it, remembering too that he had knocked it down in temper. He probably could have sold the cottage cheap as well to Tommy Parkinson, now he thought about it.

"Anyway, you won't be in any fit state to do up a cottage, now you've number three baby on the way. Have you given any thought to what you'll do after the birth?" Geoffrey changed the subject.

"Yes, three kids under school age," Linda commented, as she popped in the kitchen to eat a piece of toast before putting on her coat. "My, my, you have been busy, Alison. I don't think you'll have time to get a job. Or you could go back to Aussie land and let your husband keep you."

"That will do Linda," her father said sharply. "I think Alison

165

already knows she has a hard road ahead of her. Anyway, you might have the same problems when you're married to Peter."

"I don't think so," she said, patting the tops of her nephews' heads as she passed them by, who were both sitting on cushioned chairs at the kitchen table. "My Peter wouldn't say boo to a goose. I've got him well trained already. See you later."

"Your mother and I have been talking, Alison," her father said, after Linda had left and the children had finished their cereal. "If you are serious about leaving Graham and bringing the children up over here, we're going to have to find a strategy. I mean, will he come over and try for custody? It costs a lot of money to go through the courts, unless you can get Legal Aid from the government."

"Then he's no chance, Dad. He's up to his neck in debt. That's one of the reasons I left him. That and the thought of being tied to him for another twenty years, once I fell for this baby. Besides, if he wants to stay in Australia, he's still got a year to go on his sponsorship and won't have the money to come over here. It's not a very nice job he's doing there though."

"Not bus driving then?"

"No, Dad, it's a place where they make pipes – Graham's just a labourer. But he used to come home covered in a kind of white powder and he started getting a cough."

"Hmm." Geoffrey was silent for a moment. "If I was him, I'd get out of the place as soon as I was able. I think he'll be storing up a lot of trouble for himself if he doesn't."

"Well, you know Graham Mason. It's always been what's best for him in the long run."

"What a pity you didn't listen to us, Alison," Catherine said sadly. "All of this could have been avoided and you could have married someone like that Andy Baxendale. Did you know he went to university to study art?"

Alison nodded bleakly. "That's why he dumped me."

"Well, we've got two little grandsons from Alison's marriage to that No Mark, Catherine, and one on the way. So we'll count our blessings and see what can be done for them. You can stay here for the birth and beyond, Alison. That's if you want to."

"Oh thanks, Dad. Thanks to both of you. I knew you wouldn't turn me away. That's why I left him, when I got the chance of coming over for Linda's wedding. It seemed too good to be true when I got the invite."

"Ah well, what's done is done," Geoffrey, to Alison's surprise, said mildly. "I've an appointment at Martin's Bank this morning and don't you forget to make that appointment at the surgery."

The cottage must have been there for well over a hundred years, Alison thought sadly, as she stood in the lane with her children later, looking through the gaps in the trees. In its place was a large glass greenhouse and there were lots of rows of vegetables growing on the large piece of land. The orchard, still standing, had been her playground; the cottage her refuge from an irate father across the years. Her sorrow at its loss threatened to engulf her, so she turned away and dashed away her ready tears.

> *The dusky world in which Nora found herself inhabiting, was constantly changing. Spirits, known and unknown, were quickly disappearing, their presence just a memory from a long time ago. There seemed to be a pull in a new direction, where the sound of gurgling water was ever present and any movement of her ghostly being seemed to guide her towards a light.*

The days sped by and Alison was kept busy. Her due date, according to the new doctor in the village was the 2nd June, so with a large donation from her father and the promise of a monthly allowance from him if there was no maintenance to be had from Graham, she and Catherine went into town to do a lot of shopping for the boys and the new baby.

"Give or take a week or so," the kindly doctor had said, looking at Alison's medical notes before him and deciding that his patient, having no particular problems giving birth in the past, could have a midwife in attendance at Redstone House, instead of being booked into Grange Mount.

That hadn't gone down well with Linda.

"My wedding is on the 20th," she shouted, almost hysterically when Alison had told her the news. "What if it's late and you go into labour on the same day as I'm to walk down the aisle? Oh my God, Alison. If you stuff up my wedding, I'll never forgive you."

Nathan started to cry and Connor climbed onto his grandfather's knee, as his aunt started ranting and raving. He missed his dad, but this nice man was a comfort and seemed to like a cuddle from him now and again.

"That's enough," Geoffrey said firmly. "Think of other people as well as yourself for once, Linda. You'll have your day, which I must say is costing a lot more than Alison's wedding did."

Linda had the grace to look guilty then. Her sister hadn't had a penny towards her wedding to Graham Mason from her dad.

Drawn as Alison was to the site of the demolished old cottage, in fact she couldn't help but spend a lot of her time standing in the lane, whilst conjuring up the picture of the old place in her mind, she was amazed one day to make a big discovery. One morning, after Geoffrey had dropped them off on Borough Road, near enough for Alison, her mother and the children to walk into Grange Road where the shops were, they came upon an art gallery at the bottom of Whetstone Lane.

Her mother, attracted to the sign in the window that said 'Exhibition By A Local Artist', and liking to support local endeavours whenever she could, insisted that they take a peep inside and take a look at the pictures there. Imagine Alison's surprise as she scrutinised the picturesque paintings of idyllic scenes around Thurstaston and Heswall, to find a picture of 'Beggarman's Cottage' displayed upon the wall. It was signed by 'Andy Baxendale'. Her Andy Baxendale. The man she had been sweet on in a different life, before she had met Graham.

Her heart soared, as she imagined the wooden framed painting hanging on the wall of her bedroom *and* knowing the man who it was painted by as well. She knew that she must have it. It was her two very special memories combined into one.

"You know he's bought a bungalow down Seaview Lane, now that he's making a bit of money from his paintings," said Geoffrey, when Alison told him about her purchase, as they drove back home. The boot of the car was full of newly bought clothes for the boys, all sorts of things for the baby and the small painting of Beggarman's Cottage, lovingly packed in cardboard by the owner of the gallery.

"That's the kind of man you should have married, Alison, instead of fellow-me-lad. I was talking to Andy's mother in the bank and she's over the moon with her new place. It has three bedrooms, a nice garden and it overlooks the fields to the Irish Sea. I heard he'd paid three thousand pounds for it."

"So, he didn't get married then?" Alison asked dully, thinking that even if they met again, Andy wouldn't want to be saddled with three children.

"No," her mother broke in eagerly. "His mother would have told me if he had. I see her nearly every week in the Co-operative store where she has a part-time job. She always asks after you, Alison. I've asked them both to come to Linda's evening do. I hope you don't mind."

"No, but I hope you didn't invite them on my account, Mother. I don't think that Andy would be interested in me, especially with two children and one on the way, but still I might get a dance or two with him."

On good days, when the sun was shining and the birds were singing merrily in the trees, Alison would walk down the lane, onto the road that led to Thurstaston and past the Heatherland Cafe, where tourists and walkers alike could enjoy scones and jam or fruitcake for afternoon tea. Then onto the common where she sat with the children on the sandstone rock. Here they would look across the sparkling waters of the Dee to the Halkyn Mountains, or far away in the distance to the observatory at Bidston Hill and she would show her boys the beauty of their heritage and hope that in their future, they would come to love it too.

Some days, she would walk up the hill to the village, with little Nathan in his pushchair and holding Connor tightly by the hand, as he was apt to wander up the drives of various houses, being a curious little fellow. Passing the Manor Garage where her father had his vehicles repaired and the chip shop across the road which used to be the Irby library and then on to the Village Hall, where a newly opened play group gave her the chance to meet old friends from her primary and grammar schools and the children could join in the fun. It was good to hear the gossip, reminisce and find out how everybody else's lives had gone.

In all that time there was no communication from Graham Mason. No letter, no telephone call, not even a birthday card for Connor who had recently celebrated his fourth birthday and it wasn't often now that Connor asked about his daddy. Nathan never asked, as he had been too little to have formed much of a bond with his father and Alison didn't care. She was happy as a pig in muck, knowing she was loved by her family.

It was the day before the doctor had predicted, when Alison, waking up with twinges and the familiar sensations that always heralded that she was about to give birth, asked her mother to telephone the midwife. The family had a strategy planned. Geoffrey was to take the children to the beach at West Kirby if the day was fine, or a trip to Chester Zoo, where if it was rainy or dull, they could shelter in the enclosures. Linda, who was quite happy not to be included in the event at all, blew her sister a kiss and hightailed it. And it wasn't long before baby Mason, a little girl this time, was born.

Her name was Moyra and her spirit, with its eternal attachment to the once standing Beggarman's Cottage and to its bountiful orchard, came happily back to live on the earth.

If you have enjoyed reading Beggarman's Cottage, Vivienne would be pleased to receive your comments on www.viviennedockerty.com via Contact Me at the top of the web page